This Very Moment

OTHER BOOKS AND BOOKS ON CASSETTE
BY RACHEL ANN NUNES:

Ariana: The Making of a Queen

Ariana: A Gift Most Precious

Ariana: A New Beginning

Ariana: A Glimpse of Eternity

Love to the Highest Bidder

Framed for Love

Love on the Run

To Love and to Promise

Tomorrow and Always

This Time Forever

Bridge to Forever

Daughter of a King

This Very Moment

a novel

RACHEL ANN NUNES

Covenant Communications, Inc.

Covenant®

Cover photo © 2001 Michel Tcherevkoff

Cover design copyrighted 2001 by Covenant Communications, Inc.

Published by Covenant Communications, Inc.
American Fork, Utah

Printed in the United States of America
First Printing: October 2001

08 07 06 05 04 03 02 01   10 9 8 7 6 5 4 3 2 1

ISBN 1-57734-934-2

Library of Congress Cataloging-in-Publication Data

Nunes, Rachel Ann, 1966-
This Very Moment/Rachel Ann Nunes
p. cm.
ISBN 1-57734-934-2
1. Widowers--Fiction. 2. Charities--Fiction. 3. Mormon women--Fiction. 4. Disfigured children--Fiction. I. Title.
PS3564.U468 T48 2001
813'.54--dc21   2001042153
CIP

Dedication

To my husband, TJ, for putting up with years of corndog dinners and pajama evening gowns.

Acknowledgements

Thanks to Angela Colvin for another great editing job, and to Maren Ogden and the Covenant Design Department for another wonderful cover.

CHAPTER 1

He stared at the letter in his hand, his mind numbed with disbelief. It was addressed to Nicole Debré. How could that be? The old familiar pain, the brutal desolation, flared to life at the sight of her name. *Oh, Nicole!*

His name was Guillaume Debré, or had been once. Now he was William Dubrey, or Bill to his friends. He much preferred Bill because William was too much like that other name and identity he had left behind in France. Bill, however, seemed far removed from Guillaume Debré— and his wife Nicole, now five years dead.

Nicole. When the memories came, as it seemed they must when he was alone, they always began at that last train ride. With her fiery death, not the life they had shared. Mostly he tried not to think about it. Young love gone awry; he should have gotten over her by now. But sometimes in the night, he would remember just a flash of the lovely girl next door, of the person she had been before he had married her and taken her to Paris for their honeymoon. On the train.

Guillaume had loved Nicole his entire life. He would always love her. And the profound pit of emptiness her death had left was the reason he couldn't continue any semblance of a life in France. So he had finished his education, immigrated to the States, and had become Bill, an entirely new person, with no past to haunt his future. France was now only a bitter memory buried deeply in his new persona. His colleagues and friends knew him as a talented plastic surgeon, an ambitious, thirty-something man on the rise. A voice tutor had eliminated all but the mere vestiges of an accent. No one suspected he had ever been anything other than the American Bill Dubrey, except his older brother Jourdain, who lived in France and exchanged cards with Bill at Christmas time.

That was why the letter in the mailbox came as such a shock. Bill had nothing to do with Nicole now, but there the letter was, addressed to her. The name stabbed into his chest, choked the air from his lungs.

Nicole! Nicole! a silent voice cried. Clutching the mail to his heart, he went inside, slamming the door behind him.

Who had written to Nicole? And why here? Why now? What did it mean? The questions flooded his brain so quickly he couldn't process them. Methodically, he set his briefcase down in the entryway and studied the envelope as he walked into the kitchen. It was a simple white mailing label. *Nicole Debré,* it read, complete with the French spelling and accent. Anyone who would have known enough to connect his name with hers, and send it to America, should have also known that Nicole was dead. He threw the letter onto the kitchen table with the rest of the mail, then picked it up again. He stared at it for another full minute before tossing it into the trash, unopened.

Hot, blind anger filled every portion of his body. *How dare they! How dare they intrude upon my life!* He snatched the letter out of the garbage and ripped it open viciously, stoking his anger and resentment. He had come too far to return to the pitiful wreck he had been after the accident. He would fight this intrusion on his calm and orderly existence. *I am no longer Guillaume, but Bill, who never knew or loved a beautiful woman named Nicole.*

Inside the envelope was a gold-embossed invitation to attend a benefit dinner—a very expensive dinner to be held in L.A. in two weeks. He barely glanced at the name of the charity as he absorbed the meaning of the yellow note inside: *I met Jourdain in France last month. He gave me your address. I didn't know you had moved to California! Keep in touch. Hope to see you at the benefit. Kylee.*

For long seconds his fury was all-encompassing. He instantly recalled Nicole's friend Kylee. She had always been involved in raising money for one charity or another, in America or in other countries over the world. The women had first met in France while Bill had been in America studying, two years before he and Nicole had married. Kylee had been Nicole's best friend and confidante while he had been away chasing his dreams.

Agony burned in his soul. Why had he waited so long to marry Nicole? If he had only known that she was going to die! Perhaps marrying her earlier would have prevented her death, or at the least given them more time as husband and wife. Tears streamed down his face. "Cursed woman," he growled, crumpling the invitation and throwing it again into the trash. "Did she think that sending it to my dead wife would capture my attention? What a cruel joke." If Kylee Stuart had been in the room at that moment, he would have strangled her—and thoroughly enjoyed the revenge.

Later that night he couldn't sleep. Thoughts of his childhood with Nicole, and playing together at the park, filled his mind. Then of her as a young woman when he stole his first tentative kiss. He tossed, he turned, and he cursed until he could stand it no more. No matter how wonderful her cause, Kylee would never again use Nicole's name to elicit money. And he knew just how to stop her.

* * * * *

Kylee Stuart looked around with satisfaction. The banquet hall was decorated with stylish paintings, sculptures, and expensive knick-knacks, all of which were part of the silent auction that would be carried on throughout the evening. Two singers, a local football star, and a comedian were present and ready to display talents or give speeches. Even the children were in a back room waiting to do their part, their misshapen faces bright with excitement.

Sixteen-by-twenty-inch pictures of those children decorated one entire wall of the banquet hall. Taken close-up against a black background, these pictures made every small feature stand out and epitomized the need that had created the Children's Hope Fund five years earlier. Only the hard-hearted could look upon their innocent faces without feeling a deep compassion and desire to help.

The delicious aromas in the air reminded Kylee to do a last minute check on the meal preparations. "Everything okay?" she asked Julius Taylor, owner of the catering business as well as head chef.

Julius nodded. "Two hundred and forty meals nearly ready to go. Don't worry, everything's taken care of."

For the hundred bucks a head I'm paying you, it ought to be, Kylee thought. At the dinner cost of five hundred dollars, that meant a profit of ninety-six thousand dollars for the Children's Hope Fund, less expenses and her meagre salary. Not a bad start. And she determined the meal was to be just that—a start. The silent auction would raise a great deal of money, but she was hoping for more straight monetary donations than for anything else. As part of her plans, a video of the unfortunate children she was trying to help would be projected onto the wall-sized screen. No one would be unmoved by the deep needs of these little ones. She cried herself each time she saw the video or talked with the children, and had channelled her own slim savings into the program. Kylee was very good at what she did, but she was even better at practicing what she preached.

Shaking out her hands to relieve the tension, Kylee walked to the door to greet the guests. They came in twos and threes, and sometimes in larger groups, but never alone. They came wearing glittering clothes and cultured smiles. They came with confidence and a benign generosity. There would be two hundred and forty guests, each holding pre-paid tickets bought from the charity. Kylee was grateful to them for their attendance and for their willingness to help the children receive new faces. Of course, a few of the charity's guests could give so much more than they would offer, but she refused to think of that. She focused instead on the tears of the children and their small misshapen faces that held so much pain. Tonight she would help at least a few more of the children applying to Children's Hope for funds that would provide desperately needed surgeries.

"Welcome. Thank you for coming," she said, nodding her head graciously and occasionally taking guests' hands in hers. She knew most of them by sight, if not by name. They had come from her mailing lists, carefully compiled and maintained over the ten years she had been raising funds for charities. There was trust involved in her relationship with these donors; she had promised them that the charities she represented were of unquestionable caliber with the lowest overhead. They could rest assured that their dollars went for the intended cause, not to overpaid administrators.

"Feel free to browse through the auction items," she invited the guests, motioning them toward the items she had worked so hard in the past month to gather from local businesses and artists. She gave each guest a program which announced not only the performers and speakers, but also listed the silent auction items and minimum bids. On the last two pages were touching stories of children the organization had helped in previous years, and of those who still waited for funding.

Standing next to her, the charity administrators, Elaina Rinehart and Troy Stutts, also greeted guests, elaborating on their aspirations to help the children. Elaina leaned toward Kylee during a brief lull, her short dark hair shining in the bright lights. "These people are perfect," she said. "They really seem to care. Troy was right when he said you were the one we should contact to raise the money. You're a wonder. I bet they love you at church fund-raisers."

Kylee grinned and whispered back, "Actually, my church doesn't really have a lot of those—except for the scouts. But you ain't seen nothin' yet. Wait till I show them the video. And then bring out the children."

"I can't wait!" Elaina giggled like a school girl.

Kylee forgave Elaina's enthusiasm; she had received similar gratitude from many of the charities she had worked with over the years. Children's Hope would finally be in a position to help children who had been waiting years for a new face and outlook on life. Neither woman had any qualms about accepting donations. The wealthy had a certain amount of money they needed to donate to charities for tax purposes, and it might as well go to theirs.

Then she saw him.

The first thing she noticed about the man was that he was alone. He had wavy black hair, cut short against his scalp, and inscrutable deep brown eyes. The tuxedo he wore was of the latest style and he carried himself with sureness and purpose. His expression was pleasant enough, but she noticed that the muscles in his jaw were tight, and twitched every so often as though his outward mask flickered, threatening to reveal an inner truth he would rather hide. But how could she possibly guess all this from a stranger's face?

Pulling her thoughts back to her duty, she smiled at him as she had the others. He took her proffered hand in his cool grip and suddenly she knew him. "Guillaume! How wonderful to see you! How long has it been?"

"Kylee." His voice was far from cordial. "How dare you use Nicole to get me here. How dare you!" As he spoke, she saw the rage and contempt emerge from behind the mask.

"What are you—" Kylee glanced down the line at the oncoming guests. The people greeting Elaina were looking her way, interested in what might come next. "Come over here and we'll talk about it." She tried to pull her hand from his tightened grasp.

He shook his head and stayed where he was. "Why? Aren't you proud of your tactics? I wouldn't be either. Using a dead woman to sell one more ticket for your charity. But that's okay, isn't it? Because it's for the children. The rest of us can go to the devil—as long as you get your money first."

Kylee watched him helplessly. "I don't understand what you mean. Please, Guillaume." She took a step backward, but he refused to release his grip.

"Kylee, what's going on?" Elaina asked with a false smile that showed all her teeth. "Do you need me to call security?"

They didn't have any security, but Guillaume couldn't know that. "No," Kylee answered. "I know him." At least she had once. But why was he acting so odd, and where was Nicole?

Nicole!

Kylee's heart seemed to skip a beat. He had mentioned a dead woman.

"Nicole," she said, unready to believe. "Where is she?" She looked past Guillaume, searching, hoping to see Nicole's attractive, eager face. Perhaps this confrontation had been a joke and Nicole was watching her even now, ready to laugh the moment away. Kylee could forgive the unseemly jest—how she had longed to be with her friend again! But only the faces of the interested guests met her gaze. Kylee turned to Guillaume, her eyes filling with tears. "Dear Lord," she muttered with a heartfelt prayer. "Is it Nicole?"

His face lost much of the fury as he stared at her. "She's dead."

"I—I didn't know." Kylee blinked hard and backed away again. This time he let her go.

Without a word to Elaina, Kylee fled the room as fast as her fitted silver gown would allow. She heard someone come after her. Unlocking the door of her temporary office, she whirled on him. "Why?" She threw the word at him like a knife.

"I thought you knew."

"You should know me better than that. I was her friend!"

His shoulders slumped and he answered jaggedly, "I was just so angry. I thought I had put it all behind me. I came to America with a new name and started a new life, and then to see her name on the envelope—"

"And someone had to pay. Is that why you attacked me?" Her voice shook with her anger and hurt, but he looked dejected, and Kylee wanted to forgive him. "How long ago was it?" she asked more gently.

"Five years. Two days after we were married. We were on the train at Port Royal when it was bombed. She burned to death. There was nothing I could do." His face was immobile, but the tears in his eyes moved Kylee more than she would have expected. She took a tentative step toward him and touched the sleeve of his suit.

"I'm sorry," she whispered.

He nodded. "I shouldn't have reacted like I did tonight. I wasn't planning on staying, but I'd like to now—to make it up to you."

"You don't have to. I understand." She wiped at the tears on her cheeks.

His lips twisted into an odd sort of smile, as though the motion pained him. "I want to. Besides, I bought a ticket. Can't let a five hundred dollar meal go to waste."

Kylee felt touched at his willingness to make things right. "Okay, Guillaume. Would you like to sit at my table?"

"I'd like that. But call me Bill, okay? Bill Dubrey."

"Oh, right. You said you had a new name."

"What about you, Kylee? Have you changed your name? Your last, I mean. Are you married?"

"No, I'm not." No use in telling him about her brief relationship with Raymond.

He said nothing further, but offered her his arm. Kylee was amazed that she could see no trace of the violent emotions she had glimpsed before. Neither the grief nor the anger was apparent in his demeanor. How could he obliterate them so quickly?

"Wait." She swiftly checked her makeup in her compact mirror and rubbed off a bit of smudged mascara. After reapplying her powder and patting her short blonde hair into place, she hooked her hand through his arm and they walked back into the banquet hall together.

Elaina and Troy were still greeting people at the door. It took Kylee only a few moments with the waiter to rearrange the seating at her table, where a few guests were already seated. "I need to welcome the rest of the people," she told Bill, after she had introduced him to the others at the table. "I'll be back soon."

He gave her a wry smile. "Take your time."

"We'll keep Dr. Dubrey company," said Mrs. Boswell. "I have a little surgery I've been meaning to discuss with him."

"Oh, you know Bill?" Kylee asked.

"Not really, my dear, though I feel as if I do. My friend Audrey has simply gushed about what he did for her." Mrs. Boswell gave Kylee a conspiratorial smile, but her voice carried to everyone at the table. "A facelift, you know. She positively looks ten years younger." She focused on Bill while her husband and the other guests continued to nibble on their appetizers. "I've asked around and you have quite a reputation, Dr. Dubrey. They say you are simply the best."

Bill smiled. "I'm glad to hear it."

Kylee excused herself and hurried to the entrance, wondering at what she had learned. She had understood that Guillaume was studying to be a doctor when she had known Nicole, though she didn't remember anything about plastic surgery. Nicole had told her that after their initial bout at separate colleges, she and Bill had rediscovered their childhood love and had become engaged. While he was off in America, specializing in one thing or another, Nicole had stayed in France delivering babies—and waiting. It had been to the hospital where Nicole worked that Kylee sent several of the pregnant charity recipients she was working with at the time. She met Nicole, and they soon became close friends. Kylee remembered Nicole's sadness at Guillaume's absence, and how she had attempted to stave off her loneliness by throwing herself into fund-raising with the organization Kylee was working for. But Guillaume had returned to France often. During his visits Nicole tended to be scarce, though on more than a few weekends the three of them had gone hiking or camping together. Kylee had liked what she had seen. He was a nice guy, and perfect for Nicole.

When Kylee had moved on to England for another fund-raiser, she was pleased to receive the announcement of their long-awaited wedding. Nicole's accompanying letter had exuded complete happiness. It was the last communication Kylee ever received from Nicole, despite four subsequent letters Kylee had sent to her in France. Kylee imagined her friend was so content with her fiancé's return and their subsequent marriage that she hadn't even thought of writing. Now Kylee knew the truth, and it hurt to think that the lively Nicole was dead. No wonder Guillaume had been so angry!

Kylee glanced at Guillaume—no, it was Bill now—and saw him conversing with the group at her table. He was obviously successful, and incredibly handsome. If not for her glimpse of the emotions he had shown earlier, she would have never guessed at his former life and the tragedy behind the mask.

When she finally greeted the last of the guests, Kylee headed for her table, leaving Elaina to officially welcome the crowd and introduce the speakers and singers who would entertain them as they ate. After the dessert had been served Kylee would make her presentation of the video and the children.

"So why haven't you married, Doctor?" Mrs. Boswell was saying as Kylee arrived at the table. "Audrey has quite the eye for you, you know. And her two kids are practically in high school, so they wouldn't be much of a bother. The fact that she's moved to the same condominium complex as you is really quite convenient. I keep telling her to chase you a bit, you know. Men like to be chased." Mrs. Boswell batted her mascara-laden eyes and Kylee felt her sympathy go out to the unfortunate Audrey, who had trusted Mrs. Boswell with her heart.

"Well, I'm afraid I'm a born bachelor," Bill said as he applied crab paste onto a wheat cracker. He met Mrs. Boswell's gaze with a direct stare. "My focus is on my work. I'm much too busy for a relationship." He took a bite of the cracker and swallowed before adding, "And I especially like to work on subjects with your potential, Mrs. Boswell. You're a perfect candidate for my latest sculpting methods."

Mrs. Boswell flushed and brought a hand to her well-endowed bosom. "Oh, I may come to see you very soon, Doctor." She elbowed her husband, who nodded with a distracted smile. Kylee had the feeling that the heavyset Mrs. Boswell did whatever she pleased, with or without her husband's approval.

Kylee slipped into the chair next to Bill just as the waiters began to serve the main course. Usually she would have mingled with the guests instead of eating, in order to personally iron out any problems that might arise. But tonight Elaina and Troy would have to handle that. She owed Bill this much. She had brought him here using

Nicole's name and then, worse, she had inadvertently set him among sharks—or at least one shark. Kylee felt she should give him as much support as she could muster.

"So how long have you been in California?" Kylee asked.

He set down his fork and looked at her steadily. "Four years."

"He studied in France, you know," Mrs. Boswell said. "And the French are simply the best at maintaining beauty, aren't they?" The other women at the table nodded. "But it's certainly good to be able to go to an American doctor," Mrs. Boswell added with a sniff. "I don't trust foreigners."

Kylee caught an amused glint in Bill's eyes, and she almost laughed aloud. What would Mrs. Boswell say if she knew Bill had been born in France as Guillaume Debré? Well, Kylee wasn't about to tell her.

Everyone was blessedly silent after the waiters delivered the food, but only for a few moments. When the talk began again, it turned to politics and the economy. Kylee only halfway listened as she studied Bill from the corner of her eye. She had known him fairly well during the two years she and Nicole had been friends, and his appearance seemed the same. There were few wrinkles around his eyes, and his hair didn't have even a trace of grey. There was something still boyish and open about him. Was that what had made Nicole love him so deeply?

Kylee sighed inwardly and forced herself to think about the speech she would make. The sooner it was over, the sooner she could help the children—and the sooner she could get away from Bill Dubrey. Her memories of Nicole were too overwhelming.

CHAPTER 2

Bill was glad when Kylee returned to the table, and that she hadn't mentioned his past in front of the *créme de la société.* She didn't even seem to hold his embarrassing outburst against him. He steeled himself to endure the dinner with outward good grace, breathing a silent sigh of relief when the insufferable Mrs. Boswell finally turned her lengthy discourses to the latest plight of the United States president rather than his own bachelorhood.

Kylee was good company. She talked easily with the guests at the table, though many were twice her age. If he remembered correctly, she would be thirty-two now. A year younger than Nicole would have been had she lived, and five years younger than Bill.

The first speaker was introduced, a comedian, and Bill enjoyed some of his jokes. Yet he couldn't relax completely. His eyes kept traveling to the pictures of the children on the near wall. Some of them had second pictures below the first, showing what the child looked like after surgery. But most had no such happy ending—yet.

When one of the singers began her first piece, Bill gave an almost audible sigh of relief. The haunting melody was much more appropriate for the evening's cause. Even the football player was properly somber as he gave a speech encouraging generous donations.

After the dessert, Kylee arose and went to the microphone, her glittery silver dress hugging her slender figure. Bill noticed that her freckled nose was slightly upturned, giving her a pixie appearance, like a mythical fairy. As if sensing his thoughts, she smiled, revealing ready dimples on her smooth cheeks. "Thank you so much for being with us tonight. For those of you who don't know me, I'm Kylee

Stuart, the fund-raising organizer for the Children's Hope Fund. Many of you have been to the fund-raising banquets I've held for other charities, and I've been very pleased with your support. As you know, I research the organizations I work for very carefully before including any of you in our projects, and I'm pleased to share that through all the years of working with deserving charities, this project has touched my heart the most.

"The children who come to the attention of Children's Hope are very desperate indeed. These are children who mentally possess all of the attributes of normal children, but whose faces—and sometimes bodies—have been terribly disfigured by birth defects or by accidents. They come from here in the United States, as well as various countries all over the world. I would like to introduce to you tonight, both in person and by video, some of these special children who have benefited from Children's Hope, and also many more we hope to help with your donations." Kylee turned, looking toward the far side of the banquet hall where someone waited to dim the lights. For a moment her fairy profile was outlined by the spotlight and her short blonde hair glistened like a halo.

Then they were plunged into darkness for a full second before the video began. The first picture appeared on the screen, a little girl against a black background. Her shiny white hair and tentative smile were overshadowed by a horribly deformed upper lip and right eye. Then with no sound, the picture faded out and another child took her place, a boy this time, with no nose. A third picture was a baby with Apert syndrome, her face misshapen, the skin on her fingers fused together and looking strangely like the foot of a baby pig. Bill knew that as she grew, surgery on her skull would be necessary to prevent mental retardation, and there would be more operations to separate her fingers and toes.

On and on the pictures flashed and faded in the still darkness. A child appeared with a sad face, scarred by vicious burns. Bill heard Mrs. Boswell gasp, and though during his training he had seen much worse, he also felt disturbed. A piercing memory of Nicole after the accident flooded into his mind. Skin burned so black he couldn't recognize her. Not even his talents could make her face flesh again—or make her heart beat. He closed his eyes briefly against the painful assault. He should never have come here tonight. He should have left the invitation in the trash and let Nicole's memory rest in peace.

Softly, an ethereal melody began, delicate strains that at first Bill thought he was imagining. Slowly the sound grew louder and the tempo increased, and he opened his eyes. The children's faces still flashed on the video screen, larger than life, but now their grotesque features faded into more pleasant and hopeful expressions that Children's Hope had been able to buy for them. The adults at Bill's table mirrored the smiles of the children. Mrs. Boswell and the other ladies dabbed at their eyes with their embroidered handkerchiefs. A soft sob came from somewhere in the audience.

The music was now full and rich, teeming with hope and happiness. Some of the children in the still pictures were laughing and the music laughed with them. Bill felt those around him relax, and the grip on his own stomach lessened.

Abruptly the music stopped, as though cut off, and words loomed on the screen: *Many Precious Children Still Need Your Help Today.* Then new pictures flashed before them, more appalling than those that had gone before. This time there was no laughter and no pleasant aftershots; there was only the mournful changing of one sad little face to the next. It seemed as though everyone in the room held their breaths.

After the last picture, the room was once more dark and silent. Then the music began as before, and the lights came on one by one. Bill knew that the show had been purposely designed to evoke the emotions he normally held in check, but even so the effect was powerful. Over the years he had seen many videos done by many different charities, but never had one touched him so profoundly.

Next, Kylee brought out a group of seven children. Bill recognized at least two from the video, but to his relief, the burned child wasn't present. Two of the little girls looked normal, or nearly so, and these were introduced first.

"I want to thank you," said one, "for being so generous. Because of people like you, I was able to get my face fixed. Thank you so much." Tears of gratitude caused her soft voice to break.

Emotion rose in Bill, and the situation only intensified when one of the other children, his face grotesque without a nose, stepped up to the microphone and spoke in faltering English. "Thank you for coming tonight. Thank you for helping me. I can't say it enough times." He sobbed quietly, and the other children followed suit, obviously brimming with hope and gratitude.

"You can make the difference for these children," Kylee said. Her voice was soft, filled with a sincere pleading. Her arms encircled two of the children and her eyes glistened, and suddenly Bill believed in her. Surely the other patrons would as well. Yet no one in the audience moved or said anything.

Bill pulled out his checkbook and wrote hurriedly. He stood, holding up the check as he had seen done at other charity dinners. "I'd like to make a donation."

"Thank you, Dr. Dubrey." Kylee's smile radiated warmth.

A waiter appeared next to Bill and relieved him of the check, taking it to Kylee. "Ten thousand dollars," she read aloud. "Oh, thank you, Doctor."

Bill froze. He hadn't expected Kylee to announce the amount of his donation. By offering his check so publicly, he had wanted to inspire other donations and perhaps make up for his previous cruel words. But to have his gift set up as a target for others to meet or beat? He certainly hadn't wanted that. Not because he was ashamed of the amount—ten thousand dollars for any charity was an impressive sum of money—but because having Kylee announce it like an auctioneer somehow cheapened his genuine interest in helping the children.

Mrs. Boswell elbowed her husband, who jumped to his feet, waving his checkbook. "Well, if the good doctor can be so generous, I think I can as well." Murmurs of assent rippled through the banquet hall. Bill heard a few people double or triple his donation and saw another round of checks, of amounts unheralded, given to the hovering waiters. Kylee glowed with the outpouring, but Bill wondered how many people felt forced into donating more than they would have ordinarily because of the amount of his contribution. Surely many of them had also bid on the silent auction items, not to mention coming up with the cost of the dinner.

Swallowing the sour taste in his throat, Bill stalked away from his table, and without a backward glance, left the building. The cool of the late October night obliterated the flush he felt on his face and calmed his nerves.

His BMW was where he had left it, a sleek black that reflected the moon and the lights in the parking lot. He gripped the wheel and brought the engine to life. Once again he felt in control. But as he drove away, a picture of the burned child came to his mind, inexplicably sparring with an image of Kylee's blonde hair shimmering like an angel's halo.

CHAPTER 3

Kylee was amazed at the flood of generosity, which reached nearly three million dollars before the night had ended. From experience she knew money would continue to trickle in over the next few weeks.

Elaina stood by Kylee with tears in her eyes, hands full of checks. "It was your wonderful video and your idea to bring the children here in person. How can we ever thank you?"

"You don't have to." Kylee had made many videos for the different charities she had represented over the years, but this video was the best. Even the man she had hired to help her edit it had cried when he watched the final version. Having a few of the children appear in person had been icing on the cake. Maybe this time she could really do some good.

Of course, Bill had sparked off the night with his donation. She would have to thank him. But where had he gone? He was nowhere to be seen in the departing crowd.

Someone grabbed her hand.

"Oh, Kylee, you didn't tell me!" Julius said as he intermittently pumped her hand and patted it. "I never dreamed there were children whose faces are so . . . I mean, you see the commercials on TV with the poor children, but these children . . . What a horrible, horrible shame!" He shook his head several times, causing the white chef hat on his head to wobble. "I will give you the money back for the dinner. No," he held up his hand, "I won't hear you say no. I want to do this to help those poor, unfortunate children!"

Kyle smiled, knowing that she would never have said no. She had learned long ago not to refuse any donation. But Julius' reaction meant that she must have hit on the perfect combination to evoke the support of the public. In all the years she had used him to cater her benefit dinners, he had never donated more than a token amount. He had never, ever gone into his own money for expenses, as he would have to if he returned the entire twenty-four thousand she had given him.

"Less expenses, of course," Julius added, as though reading her mind.

Now that sounds more like Julius. "Of course," she returned. It was still a generous offer. And maybe she had a chance at getting Elaina and Troy to put the video on TV as a commercial for the charity. If it was as touching as everyone said it was, the television coverage would make much more than she had tonight with the cream of her charity lists. Of course she would have to edit it down from the five minutes it was now.

Kylee collected the checks from Elaina and Troy. She would have to make out receipts and send them with gold embossed thank-you cards before handing the money over to Children's Hope. But she could do that later.

She put the checks into her portable safe in the small office where she had talked with Bill. On the floor near the desk a white handkerchief caught her eye. It was still folded, but the top layer was wrinkled as though someone had used it to wipe their eyes. *Who has been in here?* She glanced around hurriedly. No one was supposed to come in this room. It was the one thing she insisted on with each organization she worked for: the building they rented for the banquets had to have a private office for her use.

She shook out the handkerchief and saw the embroidered initials *WD*. "Ah, William Dubrey," she said in relief. Bill must have dropped it when she was checking her makeup. Abruptly, Kylee remembered Nicole's horrible death and tears stung her eyes. She didn't throw the handkerchief away as she had planned, but clutched it tightly to her chest, feeling a deep loneliness. After several minutes, the grief faded and Kylee was able to function again. She tucked the handkerchief in her purse, picked up her small safe and other belongings, and left the room.

Troy and Elaina walked with her to her old Camry. "We wouldn't want someone to jump you in the dark," Troy said with a laugh. "All that money could be pretty tempting. You know, a life of luxury on the beaches of Brazil or something."

Kylee shivered in the crisp night air. It was much colder than she expected for late October, and she wished she had brought her full-length coat. "Well, don't you worry. I'll get it all to the bank and into your account first thing Monday morning. Then I'll fax you over the list of expenses. Of course, there'll be more donations over the next few weeks, and I'll be sure to make an accounting of those as soon as I've collected everything."

"I can't wait to see the final amount." Elaina's blue eyes sparkled. "All these years Troy and I've been trying so hard to raise the money on our own. But we should've used a professional fund-raising organizer all along. We're deeply indebted to you."

Kylee was accustomed to gratitude, but Elaina's was more profuse than most. The records of Children's Hope's dealings since it began five years ago most likely explained the reason. Kylee had seen for herself the paper trail of how they had scraped by only well enough to help a few children each year. Both Troy and Elaina held other jobs to pay their personal expenses. This last discovery was the deciding factor for Kylee in agreeing to represent them.

"See you soon." As Kylee drove off in her blue Camry, she saw Troy and Elaina begin talking, his blond head bending toward hers in a manner more personal than Kylee had ever witnessed between them. Had they become involved? She knew that Troy had been separated from his wife for six months awaiting a divorce and that Elaina was unmarried. Logically, it would be natural for them to be drawn to one another. Both were attractive; both loved and worked for the same thing. Kylee was grateful to be a part of making their shared dream come true.

She had nearly reached her home in Glendale when she remembered Bill. There was a man whose dream had been utterly destroyed through no fault of his own. How had he endured these last few years alone in a world where no one could share his grief? Why had he left France and his family?

With one hand still on the steering wheel, Kylee took out the handkerchief and brought it to her face. It smelled of spicy aftershave. Heart thumping loudly, she brought the car to a stop and opened the safe. After a few minutes of searching through the checks and promise notes, she found Bill's check. The address was located about an hour away in Newport Beach, but she could make it before midnight. *Why did he leave without saying goodbye?*

She stopped by her apartment to put the checks in her more secure alarmed safe. Back in the car, she consulted her *Thomas Guide* to locate Bill's address. Following the map's directions, she took the 5 to the 55 until it ended in Newport Beach. But when she arrived outside the group of condominiums near the address on Bill's check, she was aggravated to see a gate blocking the entryway. *Rats, a gated community.* She should have known; Newport was filled with such exclusive residences, and Bill was, after all, a well-to-do plastic surgeon. Now she would either have to jump the six-foot fence, ring Bill on the call pad next to the gate, or give up and go home.

Kylee never gave up easily, especially after driving such a long way, so that left two choices. Or one really, because she wasn't about to give Bill the chance to brush her off. So she parked the car off to the side of the road and began to climb the fence—not an easy feat in her tight dress. She had to pull the sequined material up to resemble a miniskirt, her face flushing in the dark. If anyone had been watching, they would have seen more than a little of her bare legs—even in the moonlight. As she climbed, her car keys dug into the soft skin of her palm. To make it worse, her flimsy dress jacket became stuck on the fence, and she had to climb back up to get it down. *Why didn't I change back at home?* But she knew why. She had been so anxious to find Bill that her clothing hadn't entered her mind.

And why do you have to see Bill? The question plagued her.

Because he had helped her at the banquet. Because he had left without saying goodbye. Because Nicole was dead, and Kylee had to be sure that Bill was all right. Because if she didn't come tonight, she might not have the courage tomorrow.

Once her dress and jacket were back in place there was still a long walk to Bill's place. Kylee peered through the dark at the address on each condo.

"Stop right there." A flashlight waved in her face and Kylee felt her heart nearly jump out of her chest. "Who are you?" the deep voice demanded, "and what are you doing here?"

"Kylee Stuart," she managed. "I'm here to see . . . to see someone." The man was closer now and Kylee could see he wore a guard's uniform and a blue jacket. He had brown hair and a stern face, but she couldn't make out the color of his eyes. To her relief, he didn't appear to have a gun.

Just my luck, a gated community with a live guard.

"Why didn't you ring at the gate?"

Kylee thought fast for an answer. "I . . . I wanted to surprise him." She took a step back. *Could she run for it?*

The guard moved closer and Kylee quickly gave up that thought. He looked as though he was in good shape, probably better than she was. His eyes traveled over her sequined dress, and Kylee blushed when she realized that he must have seen her climb the gate. "Well, you don't look like a criminal so I won't call the police—this time. Come on. Let's take you back to your car."

No! That wasn't what Kylee wanted at all.

She put a hand on his arm. "Look. I need to see my friend. Please."

"It's against the rules."

"Couldn't you just bend them once?" Kylee pleaded.

"I could lose my job," he said, but his voice was less stern.

Kylee pushed. "I won't let you. I promise. I'll take full responsibility. Just let me go to the right place and see if he lets me in. If he doesn't, I'll leave with you."

The guard hesitated.

"Please. I just found out tonight that his wife died. She was my friend." Kylee was accustomed to being persuasive, but felt a qualm of guilt about using Nicole this way—even though it was the truth.

The guard relented. "Okay then. I'll watch from a distance."

"Thank you so much."

The guard helped her find Bill's condo, but when they arrived she was shaking with cold and nervousness. The hand she lifted to ring the doorbell faltered. *It's near midnight now,* she thought. *What if he's sleeping? No, he didn't leave too much earlier than I did, and after the tense way he acted, I doubt he could be asleep. And if he is, he can get up. I can't be coming out here again. And it's not as if he has small children I might wake with the bell. Besides, there's that guard watching me. And I might die with the cold soon. I guess I really have gotten too used to hot California summers. I forgot how cold it gets in October. Oh, why do I feel I have to rescue every troubled soul?*

Kylee firmly pushed the white button. There was no answer so she jabbed at it again. *I guess he's not home.* She had turned to go back down the walk when the door opened. Bill appeared in a sliver of light, wearing a black silk robe. His tousled black hair was wet and when she approached his eyes looked red, as though he had held them under the shower for a long time. Kylee did this too, on those rare moments when she thought about Raymond and their brief, tempestuous marriage. The water made the red eyes explainable when tears weren't supposed to be an option.

Bill's eyes widened in surprise. "Kylee?"

"Uh, yeah." Suddenly she was speechless. She, the woman who could normally talk rolls of money out of the hardest of billionaires. It didn't make sense.

"Do you know what time it is? Never mind, come in out of the cold. You look like you're freezing." Bill backed away and opened the door wide. With an inconspicuous nod at the guard, Kylee gladly headed for the light, sighing as the warmth inside the condo rushed out to embrace her.

"In here," Bill said, leading the way to a comfortable sitting room. "Do you want a blanket? Your lips are kind of blue."

"It's not really cold out there. Compared to my hometown in Minnesota this is a heat wave. I'm fine." She set her car keys on the coffee table.

He laughed. "You don't look fine. Sit down and put this blanket on you. I was just going to make hot chocolate. Do you want some?"

His words reminded her of how many times she and Nicole had shared hot chocolate in France. Nostalgia clogged her throat and she nodded. At least with him out of the room, she could regain her composure.

Bill left and Kylee scanned the sitting room. Covering most of one wall was an enormous cherry-finished entertainment center. This was filled with a large-screen TV and a stereo system with a half-dozen speakers. On the middle of another wall was a full-size fireplace, set for a fire, but unlit. Not a single snapshot or knickknack stood out on the dark mahogany mantle. The rest of the room was sparsely furnished with a brown leather couch, a matching chair, and a coffee table stacked with books and magazines. The only picture in the room was an amateurish charcoal drawing of a young couple. The portrait hung in a dark frame next to a shelf of books that reached from the floor to the ceiling. There were no other furnishings or pictures of any kind. If she hadn't known him before, she would never have believed that this was a man whose apartment in France had been covered with drawings of nature scenes and portraits that he had sketched himself on the many hikes he had taken with Nicole. Bill had obviously eradicated his former life from his present, and Kylee's appearance here was most likely resented.

Kylee looked at the handkerchief she clutched in her hand, and wished she hadn't come. She stood and crossed the room to study the charcoal portrait more closely, and it was then she noticed that all the books on the shelves were written in French. Maybe Bill hadn't erased the past as thoroughly as she had thought.

Chapter 4

Bill was glad to escape from Kylee and gather his thoughts. He wasn't prepared to talk with anyone tonight—especially to someone who knew the truth about his life. At the same time he found himself glad it had been Kylee at the door instead of any former patients or colleagues that he had dated over the last few years. They had a way of turning up at his house at moments when they were least expected. He had soon learned that each was searching for something he couldn't give—the vital part of his heart that had died with Nicole. He couldn't love any of them with any degree of true emotion, and after experiencing real love, he found he couldn't settle for cheap imitation. Still, in the last year he had tried to get out more, and rumor had it that he was becoming a ladies' man. Only he and the women he dated knew the truth—that he was the perfect gentleman. A bit cold and remote, perhaps, but always a gentleman.

He put the milk on to simmer and went upstairs to his master suite. It occupied the entire top floor, and had been equipped with every luxury—a deluxe bathroom with a dual shower and jetted tub, an exercise room, a spacious balcony, a window seat, and even a mini-bar. But it was studiously uncrowded with furniture or accessories. He had once planned to make the empty exercise room his studio, but his recent art had been focused not on drawing, but on fixing the flaws people found in their bodies. He saw it as using the same skills in a different medium. He was good at what he did, and satisfied with his life. He didn't need his drawings to be complete.

Discarding his silk robe, he pulled on a pair of khaki pants and a long-sleeved T-shirt before hurrying back to the kitchen. He placed the pot of hot milk, cups, and containers of different chocolates onto a battered wood serving tray. *Not so bad for a bachelor,* he thought.

A sudden, unpleasant thought forced its way into his brain. Had Kylee come to ask him to perform surgery for Children's Hope? He remembered the pleading faces of the deformed children and felt his stomach tighten. Their innocence reminded him too deeply of Nicole, of her screams that day and his utter helplessness. Those children would be like Nicole, trusting and believing in a God that did not exist and could not save them. No, he couldn't perform any miracles for them. He had given them his money, but beyond that he didn't want any part of it.

Shaking off the feeling of dread, he walked into the sitting room to see Kylee studying the charcoal portrait on the wall next to his books. She started as he entered, and the blanket around her shoulders dropped to the floor. Her silver sequined dress reflected the light. There was something about the way her green eyes gazed up at him so startled and unassuming. How long had it been since he had seen anyone look that way? The women he had been dating were full of assumptions and plans. No innocence there.

Maybe she hadn't come to use him.

"Interesting," she said, inclining her head toward the drawing.

"Not very good, but it's the only one I have of my parents."

"Did you draw it?"

For a moment Bill said nothing, completely taken aback by the fact that she had once known him well enough to ask the question. That had never happened in America. "Yeah," he said finally. "I was ten. I never thought to make another one." *Now it's too late,* he added silently.

Bill pushed aside a stack of magazines and set the loaded tray on the coffee table. Kylee picked up the blanket from the floor and returned to the couch. He noticed she didn't put the blanket on again, and that her lips were no longer blue.

He sat on the couch, leaving a big space between them, and began spooning chocolate into his milk, motioning for her to do the same. "So what brings you out here so late?" He tried not to grit his teeth as he spoke.

"Well, I wanted to thank you." She smiled wryly. "And to bring you this." She held out her hand to reveal a crumpled handkerchief.

Bill felt himself relax. He gave her a smile. "Any man who can afford to give ten thousand dollars to a charity can also afford to buy a new handkerchief."

"I know," Kylee said, amusement thick in her voice. "The truth is . . . Well, I was worried about you, and I wanted to see how you were doing."

Out to rescue another person, Bill thought. *Some things never change.* Still he waited for the real reason she had come. She couldn't be as innocent as she appeared.

"But mostly because I wanted to thank you." Kylee finished mixing her chocolate and took a sip. "Your donation set off a lot of wonderful things tonight. It's always the first one that's difficult, you know. Some organizers actually put a few plants in the crowd to elicit responses, but I never have. I want it to be real. Besides, the children spoke for themselves."

"They did," Bill agreed. "But I found it rather odd that you would announce the amount of my donation to the entire crowd."

Kylee stiffened at the sharpness of the words. "But I thought that's why you gave it to me. People always want recognition."

"Why? So that they can intimidate others into donating? To top their offer?" He knew his voice was bitter, but he didn't care. "Well, I don't want that kind of recognition. I don't want to force others into donating."

Her cup clinked onto the table. "Forced into donating? Forced into donating? Don't be ridiculous, Bill! These people are multimillionaires. They use more money on a weekend shopping spree to Europe than they donated tonight. They aren't babes in the woods that I'm taking advantage of. These are grown adults with enough business savvy to run entire corporations. They knew what they were getting into when I invited them tonight. It was a charity dinner, and they expected to be asked for money. And they knew darn well how much they could give—if I showed them a good reason. So I did. We raised nearly three million dollars. Three million! With more promised. Some of them have asked for the video I made of the children to show their friends. And I'm going to put it on TV." She sat on the edge of the sofa now, face flushed and green eyes flashing indignantly. "This is going to change lives, Bill. Children's lives. I've done something good!"

His irritation diminished in the face of her vehemence. "Okay, okay," he said, "you have me convinced. I guess you're probably right about these things. I mean, what do I know? I usually donate through the mail."

The red color in Kylee's face faded. She removed her flimsy jacket, picked up her hot chocolate, and settled back on the sofa. "Yeah, well there aren't many people like you. Most want to be recognized for their donations. Take one of the guys who gave us a hundred thousand dollars tonight. He just had to come up to the podium himself to make a plug for his corporation. And I'll bet he sends a photo to the newspaper reporter we had there."

Bill picked up the handkerchief Kylee had dropped on the table. "I know you mean well, Kylee, but . . ."

"You're not comfortable with asking people for money. Well, I wasn't either at first. But then I discovered that there are too many people out there who need help but who cannot ask for themselves. That's why I do it for them."

Bill felt absorbed by the intensity with which she spoke, by her obvious dedication. Though they looked nothing alike, she reminded him in that instant of Nicole.

"What's wrong, Bill? Why are you staring at me like that?"

"It's nothing," he answered, waving his hand in the air between them.

Kylee contemplated his actions without speaking. Then she set down her mug and scooted closer to him. "I loved her too," she said. "I guess that's really why I'm here. And I feel guilty. I never even tried to contact her after those first letters I wrote. I was just too busy."

"You were in another country," Bill said dully.

"I was in and out of Paris for the two years I knew her. That never stopped me from keeping in touch." She paused, her eyes locking onto his so firmly that he couldn't look away. "I was her friend. You were her husband. I should have been there for you. I should have been there to mourn her loss. I'm so sorry. Can you ever forgive me?"

The pain in Bill's heart was aching, agonizing. He wanted nothing more than to be alone with his memories, but the tears in Kylee's eyes begged for comfort. "It's all right," he forced himself to say. "I forgive you, though I don't see the need. I should have married her long before I did. Then maybe none of it would have happened."

"Oh no! You can't think that! Nicole was happy doing what she loved to do. Doctoring people, delivering babies—new miracles into the world. If she had been unhappy with your relationship, she would have asked you to stay home instead of going to America to continue your studies. She knew it was important to you, so she was content to wait. You must believe that. Wasn't she always honest with you?"

Bill let his head drop to his hands. "I just don't know. I don't know anything anymore. And I don't want to talk about it."

Kylee grabbed his hands, forcing him to look at her. "I know it hurts, but what about the good times? Remember those trips you used to take up to the mountains? I'll never forget the day I went with you to the lake. Remember how you threw water at Nicole and she tipped the boat over to get you back?"

Despite his suffering, Bill smiled at the memory. "You two made me drag the boat to shore all by myself. My arms felt like rubber for hours. It's been a long time since I thought about that day."

"Me too, actually. Do you remember the s'mores I roasted over the fire?"

Bill snorted. "They were certainly better than that stinky fish Nicole caught."

"Yeah, you never did like fish, did you? And I don't like fish either. That was why I brought the bread. Nicole was determined to make fish lovers out of both of us, but I didn't want to starve." Kylee's laugh penetrated the numb part of Bill's heart.

"I never did thank you for that."

"You didn't have to. You and Nicole were my friends when I needed some. I wanted to contribute in any way I could to that friendship. As sort of a payment, I guess."

Now Bill's hands gripped hers. "No need. You did so much already. You were her friend when I was here studying. She talked of you all the time."

"Those were good times," Kylee said. "What came after . . . I . . ." She trailed off.

They fell silent, but it was a comfortable silence, one that didn't send sharp pains through Bill's gut. He wondered fleetingly if the mind-numbing loss and agony after Nicole's death would have been different if Kylee—or someone like her—had been there to mourn Nicole with him. But Nicole's parents lived far away, and Bill's own parents had died years before. His brother Jourdain had been there, of course, but he was soon wrapped up with the woman who would become his wife. Jourdain had found religion as well in the Mormon Church, and had tried to use the doctrine to help Bill, but Bill had wanted no part of it.

"Where have you been these past years?" Bill asked Kylee now, unable to keep the question in. "I mean, have you been fund-raising all this time?"

Her smile dimmed, and for an instant he thought he saw a pain as deep and far-reaching as his own. "I've been fund-raising," she answered, her voice hollow. "All but for about six months. I was married briefly, but it didn't work out."

Bill knew there was much more, but didn't feel he had the right to invade her privacy. Her revelation answered his questions as to why she had never again tried to contact Nicole. She had obviously been occupied with her own problems.

"All these years, I thought you two were happy," Kylee continued. "I really did." Her hand glided along his bare arm, soft and comforting. "If I had known, I would have been there."

He placed his hand over hers. "I know that now. Thank you."

After another brief silence, Kylee withdrew her hand and slid back to her side of the couch. Bill was relieved to have his own space returned to him, and yet . . .

"Well, I guess I'd better go and let you get to bed," Kylee said. "We can't have you falling asleep during your surgeries, can we?"

"I don't do many surgeries on Sunday." He suddenly didn't want her to leave. Despite his dread that she would ask for something he was unprepared to give, her presence had filled the loneliness he endured daily.

Kylee laughed and colored slightly. "Oh yeah, that's right." She scanned the room, as though searching for a way to change the subject. "It's a really nice place you have here. A little bare, but very spacious and open. Tell me, do you still draw? Where are all your drawings? You know, for a while there, I thought you might give up medicine for the arts."

"Not a chance, it was always just a hobby."

"You know, those children could use a plastic surgeon," Kylee said. "I mean they have someone already, but I don't know his qualifications.

And if I raise the funds I think I will with the TV ads, we'll need more doctors."

Bill choked on his drink, and felt himself grow pale. For a brief instant he heard Nicole scream, and in his mind he saw the burned child in Kylee's video. "No," he said shortly. "I can't be involved. I have too heavy of a load. I can't help."

Kylee stared at him as though surprised at his terseness, but she didn't pursue the matter further. "Okay. So where are your drawings? You do still have them, don't you? Will you show them to me?"

Bill nodded, though he didn't want to show them to her or see them himself. But he felt obligated to Kylee for his outburst. Besides, he would do anything to change the subject. "Come on." He led her into the corridor and up the stairs, giving her the grand tour along the way.

"This is nice," she said. "But what's this room for?"

"It's supposed to be an exercise room."

She laughed. "Everyone knows doctors are too busy to exercise—unless it's tennis or golf."

"Ha! You'd be surprised. About a half a dozen surgeons I know go every night to the gym."

"You're a member of a gym?"

"Yeah, but I don't go much." Bill headed for the closet.

"You know, this would make a good studio," Kylee commented.

Bill smiled, not admitting that he had once shared the same notion. He tugged at a box in the corner of the closet, bringing it to the center of the room. Then he brought out a stack of larger drawings that he had propped up inside the closet between two pieces of thick cardboard. He blew off the dust before taking out the first drawing.

"Oh, these are beautiful, Bill! Just like I remembered. Look at this one. It's Nicole exactly the way she looked after catching that big fish. It's perfect!"

"She hated that drawing. She said she looked too smug."

"But that was how she looked that day." Kylee's green eyes were bright and sparkled with amusement. "Remember how she teased us about not catching any?"

"I didn't use a hook," he confessed, with a laugh. "I thought if we didn't catch any, we could make do with your bread."

"Good one. I never thought of that."

They thumbed through the charcoal and pencil drawings, laughing as they remembered adventure after adventure. Bill hadn't looked at the drawings since he had packed them away after Nicole's death. He had thought it would bring too much pain. Yet with Kylee there it was bearable, and even comforting. For the first time, he felt as if Nicole were near, though he knew she was gone forever. Then the moment was shattered.

"Who's this?" Kylee pointed to a drawing of a young girl with long dark hair and expressive dark eyes.

Bill's smile faded as he recognized the drawing he had done five years earlier, the only one he had drawn since Nicole's death. There was more to the girl in the drawing than innocence; there was something ethereal, or perhaps fragile. He admitted to himself that he had captured his subject perfectly.

"Pauline."

"Who is she? She looks like an angel."

"She was—if you believe in that sort of thing." For a moment Bill debated whether or not to say more. "Her brother was caught in the subway bombing in Paris, the one that took Nicole's life. Her parents managed a café nearby and came running when they heard the noise from the bomb. Their children were coming home from school on the train and they all made it out safely—except their oldest boy who got trapped in the debris when he went back to help someone."

"What happened to him?"

"He sustained kidney damage and nearly died, but he recovered and eventually received a transplant."

"How did you come to sketch her?" Kylee looked again at the drawing. "She's so serious, and yet one can see the love in her eyes."

"She saved my life that day." Bill heard his own voice as though from far away. "I was kneeling on the ground by Nicole's body, knowing that my life had ended. I felt so alone. Alone enough to lie down beside Nicole and die. But then this little girl runs up to me and throws herself in my arms, hugging me and saying words I couldn't even understand because I was in such shock. She cried with me as though my pain were her own, and suddenly I knew I was going to live. It might not be much fun, but I was going to live.

"Pauline's mother and aunt were helping out with the other bombing victims, even while awaiting news about their own son. I helped them get a lady to an ambulance and then I went back to Nicole. I don't remember much else of that day, just Nicole and little Pauline's face. I never saw her again. I drew this from memory." He glanced at Kylee and found her staring at him, tears in her eyes. "I did send my brother later to her house with Nicole's love ring, the one I gave her our last year in grade school. I wanted Pauline to have it. She had as much love inside her as Nicole had." Bill's lips twisted in a wry smile. "Funny thing is that Jourdain met Pauline's aunt that day, and not long after that he joined their church and married the aunt."

"He married this girl's aunt, yet you never saw her again?"

He nodded. "That was when I left France." He wished he could stop there, but he couldn't. "It wouldn't have mattered. Pauline's dead now. Two years ago, Jourdain sent me back the ring."

"How?" Kylee's touch on his arm was gentle.

He sighed wearily. "AIDS. She was born HIV positive. Her parents died just after she was born and she and her sister were adopted by their aunt and uncle—their other aunt, not the one Jourdain married. They had three or four other kids already, including the boy who was hurt in the subway. When they adopted her they knew it was only a matter of time until Pauline died."

"I'm sorry," Kylee said. "I guess that explains the look on her face. She is an angel."

Bill didn't reply, but turned to the next drawing, a lake scene. "This was Nicole's favorite."

"It's beautiful."

Slowly Bill's peace returned. He found Kylee's presence intoxicating, and wondered at the emotions inside him. Already he had shared more of himself with her than with anyone since Nicole. Her laughter was infectious and her concern genuine. He didn't want the evening to end, despite the painful memories many of the drawings evoked.

"I know it's terribly late, but how about I get us a snack?" he asked when they were nearly through the box of drawings.

"I am hungry," she admitted. "As good as Julius' food is, I'm always too nervous to eat much at those banquets."

Bill climbed to his feet. "You didn't look nervous."

"Well I was." Her eyes glistened as she stared at a portrait of Nicole in her doctor's smock, holding a newborn infant. She met

Bill's gaze. "Thank you so much for showing me these. This might sound corny, but I somehow feel redeemed for not being there. Like I'm able to say goodbye."

Tears pricked at the back of Bill's own eyes. "You're welcome." He left the room quickly, allowing them both time to compose themselves. He knew exactly the right snack to make. It was a little sweet, but it would fit the moment. Now if only he had all the ingredients.

* * * * *

Kylee smiled gratefully as Bill left the room. Here she had come to help him mourn Nicole and she was the one who was crying. She wiped her tears and thumbed through a few more drawings. Most were nature scenes, but there were many portraits as well. Nicole was often the subject, and each drawing of her told Kylee how much Bill had loved her. Many of the early ones, when Nicole was the little girl next door, were crude, but the later ones were very good. If he had cared to, Kylee was sure Bill could have done well in the art world. But then, Kylee believed that most people would be good at anything they put their minds to. It was simply a matter of combining determination and dedication: qualities her ex-husband Raymond had never possessed. She discovered too late that he wasn't able to face trials without crumbling. Looking back, she knew it was inevitable that he would leave her. The memory brought a terrible anguish, overshadowing the sweet thoughts of Nicole.

Taking a deep breath, she picked up a drawing of a woman sleeping on a couch. She blinked twice and held the paper closer. It was her! Kylee instantly recalled the night it must have been drawn. She had been at a benefit dinner and had been too tired to drive home. Nicole's apartment was closer, and since Kylee had a key, she had opted to stay at Nicole's as she had often done before. Nicole was out with Bill that night, who was back from the States on a school break, but Kylee knew her friend wouldn't mind. She had sat down to watch a little TV, but her eyes grew heavy, and she had fallen asleep on the couch. Bill must have brought Nicole home sometime later and seen her there. Had he gone right home to his brother's apartment and drawn the scene from memory?

In the drawing, Kylee was lying on her back, one arm above her head, face relaxed, her features softened by shadows. Kylee thought she looked more beautiful than in real life, and her heart took on a curious rapid beating. Did Bill see her that way? Then again, perhaps she had been more beautiful back then, before Raymond had stolen her belief in love. Certainly she had been more innocent and carefree. Maybe that was what made the drawing so special.

Pleased but embarrassed, Kylee hid the drawing under the stack she had already seen. She stretched out on the floor to uncramp her legs while she waited for Bill. Exhaustion settled over her. For a brief moment she closed her eyes.

* * * * *

After rummaging through his entire pantry for a half-full sack of marshmallows, Bill finally returned to the room with his old battered serving tray full of warm, toaster-oven s'mores. But only to find Kylee asleep on the floor. In repose, she looked much younger than her thirty-two years. She looked beautiful and vulnerable, though a bit more guarded than when he had known her in France. Had her husband done that to her?

He gingerly removed her silver high heels. When she didn't stir, he picked her up gently, carried her to his room, and laid her on the bed. As he tucked several of his quilts around her, he thought she would wake, but she sighed and snuggled deeper into the warmth of the bed. That she didn't stir further told him how exhausted she must be. He watched her for a moment before leaving with a blanket under his arm. Tonight he would sleep on the couch.

Chapter 5

Kylee awoke in the morning with a general sense of confusion. Where was she? Then she remembered. "Oh, no," she muttered. What had Bill thought about her falling asleep like that? Kylee pushed off the blankets, feeling the cooler air of the room assail her bare legs. The sequined gown had worked its way up to her waist and she pulled it down, frowning at the wrinkles. She hoped they would come out with dry cleaning.

She went into the master bathroom to splash water on her face and rub the smudged mascara from beneath her eyes, wishing she hadn't left her purse in the car. The extra set of makeup she kept in it would have come in handy. Oh well. She ran her hands quickly through her short blonde hair, restoring it to some semblance of order. Now to find Bill and take her leave. There was a lot she had to do before church that morning.

Peeking into the exercise room, she saw the drawings still lying on the floor. A tray of foil-wrapped objects and a tea kettle of milk had been set nearby. "S'mores!" The milk was likely unusable, but the s'mores . . . She picked one up, opened it, and tasted the contents. They were cold, but with a little toasting, they might still be edible. Carrying the tray, she walked down the stairs and into the spacious kitchen where she found a toaster oven. "Perfect." She turned it on and slipped the s'mores inside.

She had seen no sign of Bill. Where was he? She headed for the sitting room and found him lying on the couch, stretching.

"Hey, sleepy head," she said. "How about s'mores for breakfast?"

Bill groaned and sat up. "Only you could eat something that sweet for breakfast."

Kylee laughed. She did have the biggest sweet tooth of anyone she knew. "Oh, come on, Bill. Try it."

"Okay, as long as it's not fish." He laughed as he said it.

"Do you have anything I could wear?" Kylee asked. "I know it's pretty, but I'm really sick of this gown. Do you know how it feels to walk like a mermaid for a whole day?"

He grinned, cocking his head back to look up at her. "I'll find you something. It might be a little big, but . . . tell you what, you pick out whatever you want."

They turned off the toaster oven and went upstairs to his closet. Kylee chose a long-sleeved striped polo that went halfway to her knees and a pair of grey sweats with a draw string. She changed in the master bathroom and when she reemerged into the bedroom, Bill smiled.

"What?"

"Nothing."

She scowled. "Tell me right now!"

"I was just thinking that you looked gorgeous in that other dress, but now you look adorable."

Kylee sighed. "Puppies are adorable. Never mind, let's get downstairs before our breakfast is ashes. Even with the oven off it might still burn the s'mores."

"Are you sure you don't want bacon and eggs? I thought all Americans ate eggs or pancakes for breakfast. Don't you know how to make pancakes?"

She smiled at him sweetly. "Don't worry. I'll make them for dessert."

And she did.

"I've never tasted pancakes so wonderful," he said, pouring a stream of syrup over a second stack of them. "You're a good cook."

She grimaced. "Yeah, it was the one thing my ex knew how to do well. He loved good food, and I learned from him. Funny thing is, I actually enjoy it. Cooking, I mean. It's therapeutic."

"Cheaper than a shrink."

Kylee pulled one leg up to her chest as she sat on her chair, leaning her arm over it to reach her food. "I hear ya."

After breakfast, Kylee glanced at his clock. "Uh-oh. I've got to get going. I have to teach Sunday School in an hour and a half. It'll take me nearly an hour to get home and I need to shower and change."

She bounced to her feet and grabbed her folded dress from the extra chair. "I'd better get out of here. Where did I leave my shoes? Okay if I return your clothes later?"

"Sure," Bill replied. "But since when did you get religious? I don't remember you ever attending any church."

"Oh, for a while." She purposely avoided his gaze. He was right; she had never frequented any church, despite Nicole's occasional invitations. "Maybe I'll tell you about it some time. But not now. I have to get going."

Kylee wasn't ashamed of her religion, quite the opposite, but she definitely wasn't ready to share her past with Bill, particularly the painful events that caused her to find religion—at least not yet. Though she should probably explain how her religion tied in with meeting his brother in France. Not that it would make a big difference to him.

"But you could shower here and wear your dress to church." He motioned toward the silver material in her hands.

She shook her head. "Not a chance. It's wrinkled. Besides, I teach a class of sixteen-year-olds, mostly boys with raging hormones. I may not be as young and beautiful as their girlfriends, but I know this dress is form-fitting, and I'm not about to endure an hour of side looks and comments. I'm their spiritual advisor, not showcase model."

Bill laughed. "I see what you mean. But I rather like that dress."

"It's designed to be liked, and I have more just like it. All glittery dress-up dresses, designed for the banquets, you know. I have to dress like the crowd, if a bit more modestly. I mean, I don't see how those women stay warm with those strapless things."

Bill's grin widened. "That's why the men wear those hot jackets—to offer them to the women. But it does seem incongruous."

"Do you want to come with me to my Sunday School class?" Kylee asked suddenly. She hadn't meant to ask, but the words burst out of their own accord.

Bill's smile faded. "No, thank you."

He offered no explanation or apology, but Kylee knew from his cool manner that she had hit on a nerve. She met his eyes without flinching and asked quietly. "What's wrong, Bill?"

He shook his head. "I don't go to church, that's all."

"But you used to." *With Nicole,* Kylee added silently.

Bill looked thoughtful, as though choosing his words carefully. "I'm an atheist now. Or as good as one. I figure if there is a being such as God that he really would be too busy to care about what happens here. I mean, Kylee, there are endless worlds out there in the universe and probably a far greater number of sentient beings. Why would an omniscient God care about something as insignificant as a human life?" He held up his hands to stop her comments. "I'm not saying that he exists, mind you. I don't think he does, but if he did, he couldn't possibly care about each living thing on those zillion worlds. What would Nicole mean to him? Or the fact that innocent little Pauline was dying such an agonizing, unfair death? Each is just one more grain of sand on a beach."

Kylee listened to his speech with a growing sadness. After Raymond had left, her Father in Heaven had been the one strengthening force in her life, the only reason she had survived at all. And to hear someone she cared about denounce God greatly upset her. "I know it seems impossible to us," she said. "But I really doubt an omniscient being deals with time and space in the same way that we do. And I'm sure He has others to help Him."

"Angels?" The word was almost mocking. "If there are angels out there, well, they would probably be a lot more concerned about one another than us lowly ants."

"Bill, don't." Kylee hated the cynicism in his voice. "I've seen His work with the people I've been involved with over the years. I know He lives and cares about us. Look at the sacrifice Jesus made for us on the cross."

"See? That's what's even more strange to me. The idea of an ultimate Atonement is ridiculous. I mean, why would a being so great and powerful care about lowly humans enough to die for them? It's beyond comprehension. I know no one who would willingly die for another. It goes against the instinct of self-preservation."

"That's just it," Kylee said. "Jesus is beyond instinct, beyond the natural man. He wasn't mortal, not as we are. He was selfless, and He always put others first."

"But why would he do such a thing? I just don't buy it."

"I can't explain it to you. It's something I feel with my heart."

An uncomfortable silence fell between them. Then Bill said

lightly, "Well, we can still be friends. But you now have five less minutes to get to your Sunday School class."

Kylee accepted his words as a truce. "Okay, but do you remember where I put my shoes?"

"They're in with my drawings. I took them off when you were asleep."

His words reminded Kylee of how years ago he had drawn her while she slept. Did he still think she was as appealing as the drawing portrayed? Why did she care? Kylee flushed and Bill laughed. "I bet you're wondering how you would explain sleeping over here last night to your Sunday School class," he said.

"I'm sure they'd understand."

He gave her a knowing smile. "Oh, sure they would. And *you'd* have to understand when they wanted to do it."

Kylee was beginning to see a new meaning to the phrase "avoid the appearance of evil." That she hadn't meant to stay the night, even under such innocent conditions, really wasn't the issue. She scowled at Bill. "I'd better get my shoes."

"I'll get them." Bill left the room. She heard him run up the stairs and down again before she made it to the sitting room where she had left her car keys. "I'll walk you to your car," Bill said at the front door. "Wait, wear one of my jackets. It's getting cold in the mornings, even for California."

Kylee put her arms into the sleeves as he held it. "Thanks."

Bill threw on his own jacket and opened the door for her. As they walked down the front walk, a beautiful red-haired woman Kylee didn't recognize charged up it. She heard Bill give a soft groan before greeting her. "Hi, Audrey."

Audrey. Audrey, thought Kylee, knowing she had heard the name recently in connection with Bill.

"Hi, Bill," Audrey said brightly. "I just slipped over here to invite you to go on a picnic this afternoon. I have the most perfect cold cuts that I bought over at Macky's yesterday, knowing how much you like them, and I know this lovely little . . ." Audrey's words faded as she stared at Kylee, taking in her oversized clothes and the folded dress in her hands. Her eyes focused on the silver sandals on Kylee's feet.

Bill put a hand on Kylee's shoulders, pulling her closer. "Audrey, this is Kylee, a very old friend of mine who I ran into last night at a charity banquet. In fact, we also met a friend of yours there, a Mrs. Boswell? Do you know her? I thought so. Well, she certainly had a lot of good things to say about you."

Oh, thought Kylee. *This is the former patient who has her sights set on the doctor.*

Bill's hand drifted down to Kylee's waist. "You remember, don't you Kylee?"

"Yes," Kylee said perfunctorily. "Mrs. Boswell did mention you. It's nice to meet you."

Bill's arm tightened on her waist, forcing her to step even closer to him. "Kylee here is the organizer for the charity. She's a marvel at raising funds for unfortunate children. Always has been."

Audrey's face drooped. "Oh." She glanced again at the gown in Kylee's hands. "It's a pretty dress."

"Kylee has to dress up for these banquet affairs you know," Bill answered.

"Bill—" Kylee began, not wanting him to continue.

"Oh, yeah, you have to get going now." He looked at Kylee as if he had just remembered. Then to Audrey he said, "She's late for an appointment. Let me walk her to her car and then we'll talk, okay?"

"It's okay, I'll get back with you. See you around." Audrey retreated down the sidewalk.

Without a word, Kylee began walking in the opposite direction as Audrey, leaving Bill behind. He had to run to catch up with her. "You weren't very nice," she told him sternly.

He looked at her, forehead wrinkling in puzzlement. "That's where you're wrong. I really like Audrey," he said. "As a person, though, not as someone to have a relationship with. I can't give her what she wants, Kylee. I can't give it to any woman. It's just not in me to give. I've tried to explain it to her, but she just takes it as a challenge. The faster Audrey gets over her infatuation with me, the sooner she can develop a trust in herself, some confidence. Then she can have a good relationship with someone else. What she's looking for now is someone to save her. That's not good. A new life takes more than just a facelift."

"She thought we were together last night." Kylee turned her

flushed face away.

"We were together."

"You know what I mean."

"I know, but you're so fun to tease. Seriously, though, it's better for her to think I'm not available. Don't worry, I'll still be her friend."

Kylee knew he was right to some extent, though she didn't approve of his methods. When her marriage with Raymond had ended, she had also been desperate for attention, for someone to take care of her. She had endured several bad relationships before she learned that Kylee was the only one who could take care of Kylee.

"Okay," she relented. "But, you know, this is my reputation at stake."

Bill sobered immediately. "I'm sorry, Kylee. I shouldn't have used you that way."

She pushed her shoulder against his playfully. "I forgive you. Just don't do it again."

"I promise." He squinted into the early morning sun. "Excuse me a minute, but how far out did you park anyway?"

Kylee groaned. "Oh, I forgot. I had to park outside the gate."

"You what? Why didn't you ring me?"

"It was getting late. I didn't want you to say no."

"Stubborn. I remember that now. You were always stubborn."

"It's a good quality, right?" Kylee raised a fist, warning him not to disagree.

"All right, all right. But how did you get over the . . . You didn't climb, did you?"

Kylee nodded wryly. "I guess the security camera got an eyeful."

"I bet it did. You better hope there were no crimes committed last night."

"Stop, Bill!" Kylee said the words, but didn't mean them. It felt good to be teased. She could almost imagine that the intervening years and all the heartbreak hadn't occurred.

They walked through the gate to Kylee's car. She opened the door.

"Got a pen and something to write on?" Bill asked.

Kylee slid into the car and opened her purse, glad to see that nothing had been disturbed or stolen. Apparently this was a good neighborhood. "Here." She shoved a pen and pad at him.

He jotted something down and handed it back to her. "It's my code for the gate. Just in case you ever need it. And my phone number. It's unlisted."

"Thanks." Kylee felt awkward now, looking up at him. They had shared so much during the past hours, but all at once there was a gulf between them. Was it Nicole? "I guess we'll be seeing you." She inserted the key into the ignition and brought the engine to life.

Bill ran his hand along the edge of the open door, his other hand resting on top of the car. "I'd like to get together again some time. In fact, I have to attend a dinner for plastic surgeons in L.A. next Saturday. I didn't want to go, but they're giving me an award or something. I'd like you to come with me. It'll make me look good."

"To fend off the ladies?" Kylee wasn't sure she wanted the role.

"Yeah, something like that. Come on, you owe me. I went to your dinner."

"I have another one in two weeks for Children's Hope," Kylee countered. "I'll make you a deal. You come to mine again, and I'll go to yours." If he was going to use her as a prop, then she could do the same.

"Do I have to donate again?" he asked with a grin.

She flipped on the heater, hoping the car had warmed up enough to thaw her feet. "Of course you do. If you can afford it."

"Okay. It's a deal. You keep the women away from me, and I'll go to your dinner and make a donation. Sounds fair." He stuck out his hand and Kylee shook it.

"Goodbye," she said.

"Kylee, just one more thing." His voice was abruptly quiet and serious. "You came here last night to thank me, but it's me who should thank you. I've never talked with anyone before about Nicole. I thought I would never want to, but it helped."

Kylee smiled gently. "You're welcome." At least she had accomplished what she had come to do.

Bill stepped back out of the way and slammed the car door shut. Kylee saw him wave as she drove away, her thoughts in a jumble.

Shaking her head, Kylee turned onto the freeway, glancing at the clock on the dash. Now she would be lucky to have five minutes to shower and change when she arrived home. Good thing her lesson was already prepared.

* * * * *

Bill watched Kylee drive away, wondering at the unfamiliar feelings in his heart. Was it because talking about Nicole lessened his pain? How had sharing his memories of her with Kylee accomplished that great feat? Was it because Kylee had also known and loved Nicole?

The words Kylee had said about Jesus kept returning to him. It was beyond his comprehension that one person would give his life for another. Bill understood the instinct of self-preservation only too well. Five years ago on the subway when the bombs had detonated and the fire had begun, he had thought solely about himself, about the excruciating pain he was experiencing as the flames engulfed them. Not even Nicole's screams of agony and terror had pulled him from his self-absorption. Only later, after his pain dimmed, had he been able to concentrate on finding his new bride. Only later had he internalized her screams—the ones that still found their way into his nightmares.

At least Kylee hadn't pestered him about helping the children after his first refusal. The last thing he needed was to have someone depend on him—or to fail again.

Shaking his head to ward off the painful memories, he walked slowly back to his condo under a rising sun that was still too weak to give real warmth to the earth. As he passed the gate, he thought about Kylee climbing over it in order to see him. The funny image cut through his memories of the burning train.

Drawing a large breath of cool air into his lungs, he laughed aloud, feeling alive and tingly. It had been a long time since his laughter had been real.

CHAPTER 6

Bill didn't feel nervous until he walked up to Kylee's third-floor apartment door Saturday evening, a week after the charity banquet. He told himself he was excited to be with her because her presence made him feel as if Nicole were near, but was that the only reason? *Calm down,* he thought. *This is just a deal we made, not a date.* Yet the anticipation of seeing her again had been building for nearly a week. He had thought about calling her—but what would he have said?

Kylee opened the door with a cheerful smile. "Bill! Come on in. I just have to get my bag. It's in my room."

He whistled appreciatively, eyeing the glittering bronze and gold dress she wore. It was long-sleeved and completely modest, but the snug fit and the design of the bronze over gold gave it the allure of a strapless dress. The warm colors set off her blonde hair and green eyes better than the silver dress she had worn before. "You look wonderful!"

She spun around for him and gave a little curtsy. "I told you I have a lot of these things. This is my favorite, though. I haven't worn it for a while." She took his arm and led him inside her living room. Unlike his condo, her apartment was small and filled with furniture, color, and life. "Look around, if you like. I'll get my purse." She disappeared down a narrow hall.

Bill gravitated toward the throng of pictures on the white-painted mantel above the pseudo fireplace. These would give him a glimpse into Kylee's life. Besides a snapshot of Nicole, Bill didn't recognize anyone in any of the pictures. Probably friends or family he had never met. Was one of the men Kylee's ex-husband? One small picture in an elaborate gold frame drew his attention: a close-up of a tiny newborn baby, eyes shut tight against the world. But there was something odd about the child that Bill couldn't pinpoint. He picked up the frame and turned it over. On the back was the single word *Emily,* and a date nearly four years earlier.

Kylee returned to the room. "I'm ready." Her smile faded when she saw what he held in his hands.

"Who's this?" he asked, sensing she didn't want to talk about it, but unable to stop his curiosity.

"It's Emily, one of the many children modern medicine couldn't save." Kylee's voice held a deep sadness. "I keep her picture here to remind me that I can make a difference in children's lives, even if I can't save them all." She crossed the room and took the picture from him, setting it down carefully on the mantel.

"She was very special to you."

Kylee nodded. "But each is special, Bill. They are truly children of God. That's why I have to help them."

He took her hand, wanting to take away her sadness. "And you're doing a great job. I mean, take that banquet last week. You collected nearly three million in one night. That's pretty good."

She took her eyes from the picture. "More has come in, Bill. And we are using it to set up a television ad campaign that I feel is going to top anything I've ever done before. We'll be able to help all of the kids on Children's Hope's waiting list, and more."

"TV ads? When do they start?"

"Today. They'll be on nearly every channel."

Bill started for the door. "Sounds like you've had a busy week."

"I'll say." Kylee opened a closet and took out a long duster that matched her dress. It didn't look very warm. "But the biggest problem I had was in convincing Elaina and Troy—the heads of the charity—to let me use a good portion of the money I already raised to pay for the commercials. They're afraid to lose what they have."

Bill helped her pull on the wrap. "But with that video, you can't go wrong." He waited for Kylee to lock her door before punching the button on the ancient elevator.

"That's what convinced them. Of course, I had to whittle the video down so that most spots will be either thirty or sixty seconds. And now I'm in the process of trying to get the news on each station to do a story on us. That way we can gain some authenticity in the public eye."

"So the people don't think you're making off with their money."

"Exactly. Several of the newspapers have already agreed to carry the full story."

"What about phone solicitation?"

"Got it covered. I have a company I usually work with. They take the lowest cut and are really good. They'll have a crew ready to answer the phones when people call in to make a donations with their credit cards."

"See, Kylee. You're amazing."

She smiled at him. "Thanks." The way she said it told him something. She wasn't thanking him for the compliment, but for getting her mind away from the baby in the picture.

"So what award are you getting tonight?" she asked as they drove to the banquet.

"Oh, Doctor of the Year or some such thing."

Her eyes widened. "Doctor of the Year? You really are doing great things, aren't you?"

"Well, they have to give it to someone. Every year we vote, and this year I came out the winner. It doesn't mean much."

"It means you're respected by your peers. To me that says a lot about who you are."

They continued to talk and joke, but avoided mention of the past. When they arrived at the banquet, Bill felt more light-headed than he usually did after a few stiff drinks. "I don't think I've laughed so much since . . ." *Since before Nicole died,* he finished silently.

Kylee squeezed his hand in understanding. "Me neither."

They showed their invitations at the door and were escorted to a table. Bill could feel the eyes around the room turn in his direction. He was well-known, but Kylee was a newcomer and his male colleagues would be curious about such a beautiful woman. The women stared too, and Bill realized that a few of the ladies he had dated would not welcome the competition Kylee presented. Of course, he didn't fool himself that they wanted anything other than his money and prestige.

Bill promptly went about enjoying the evening. Even when he had to accept his award for being chosen Outstanding Doctor of the Year. "I don't deserve this any more than any of you," he said, briefly addressing the audience. "But I am honored. Thank you."

The announcer joined him at the podium. "And as you all know, there is a cash sum of twenty thousand dollars that goes with this award to be donated to Dr. Dubrey's favorite charity. Can you tell us yet, doctor, which that will be?"

"Yes," Bill answered without reflection. "It's the Children's Hope Fund. For those of you who haven't heard of it, they're a charity that gives disfigured children new faces. They're really doing miraculous things for these children, and since I know the organizer personally, I know the money is going for the children and not to expensive overhead. Watch for the newspaper coverage and for their TV ads beginning tonight. I'm sure you'll all want to be involved in this worthy project. Thank you again."

He returned to his seat amidst vigorous clapping. Kylee leaned over and kissed him on the cheek. "You were wonderful! Why didn't you tell me?"

Bill grinned. "Wasn't it better as a surprise?"

"Yes, I guess it was. Thank you."

"Like I once heard a lady say, there is money to be donated and it might as well be to her."

Kylee colored. "Ouch. If we weren't in a room full of people, I'd stick my tongue out at you."

"Then why don't we get out of here?" he asked, taking a sip of wine. He noticed that Kylee hadn't touched her glass. Had she given up alcohol? The only other person he had known who had done that was his brother, and that was when he joined his new church.

"But should we leave so soon?"

"All that's left is the after-mingling, and if we're gone they can talk about us more easily."

Kylee's shoulders shook in a silent giggle. "Okay, let's go."

They arose, but before they could take a step, a small posse descended upon them. Bill grimaced and whispered, "Remember our deal." The approaching women were both competent plastic surgeons and attractive, and he had gone out with each of them once—when they had asked. But he had felt uncomfortable with their designs on his future. Neither of them had Kylee's wholesome aura.

"Leaving so soon?" Sandra drawled. She was the more outgoing of the two.

Bill felt glad when Kylee stepped closer to him and put her arm through his. "Yes, we have to be going," he replied. "We have another important engagement tonight."

"At least introduce us to your friend." Merriam's hostile eyes looked Kylee over from head to toe, assessing her competitive value like a prize fighter entering the ring.

"Sandra, Merriam, this is Kylee Stuart. Kylee, this is Sandra Burnheart and Merriam Gotsby." He wished he could leave it at that, but etiquette dictated that he elaborate. "They are both wonderful plastic surgeons here in town. We've had the pleasure of getting to know each other through the conferences we've all attended."

"Are you a doctor, too?" Sandra asked.

"Actually, I organize fund-raisers," Kylee said. "I work with different charities to help them meet their monetary needs, especially children's charities."

"Oh, how sweet." Sandra was obviously unimpressed.

"Yes, isn't it?" Kylee answered, not retreating at the condescension in the other's voice. "In fact, if you wish, I'll send you a copy of the video I've done for Children's Hope. I think you'll find it . . . interesting."

Merriam glanced at Bill. "Is that the charity you talked about?"

"Yes, it is."

"Oh, so that's how you know each other." Sandra sounded relieved.

Bill put his arm around Kylee. "Actually, Kylee and I are old friends. Now if you'll excuse us . . ."

"Go ahead and send your video," Sandra told Kylee. "Bill can tell you where. He's been to my house before." With a pair of false smiles the women turned away, allowing them to escape.

"Wow," Kylee said as they slid into the comfortable seats of Bill's BMW. "Do you go through that a lot?"

He sighed. "Unfortunately. There aren't many men who are single these days. All the most eligible ones are snatched up. There's not enough to go around. And the more educated the women are, and the more money they make, the more difficult it becomes for them to find a good match."

"Don't I know it," Kylee said. "But even so, you do seem to attract more than your share of hangers-on." She rubbed her arms, hoping to bring warmth to her suddenly cold heart. "You know, when Raymond learned that I didn't keep the full percentage that I should from raising money for the charities, he just about went ballistic. He thought by marrying me he could take a permanent vacation. I wouldn't let him."

"Is that why you broke up?" Bill kept his eyes on the road as he spoke, hoping the question wouldn't feel threatening to her.

Kylee gave a long sigh. "One of the many reasons. I guess I should have tried to get married when I was younger, before all the good ones were taken. But I had my dreams."

"Worthwhile dreams," Bill said. "And they wouldn't have interfered with your finding someone eventually."

"I know. It's just hard to be lonely sometimes."

"I hear you. But it's good to have a friend." He took one hand from the wheel and held it out to her. She put her hand in his and for a long time neither spoke. Then Bill said, "I know a great movie that's playing at Universal City Walk. Want to see it? Or would you rather go home?"

"The movie," she answered. "But I can't be out too late. Remember I have to teach—"

"Sunday School tomorrow. I know. I remember."

Bill enjoyed the movie and being with Kylee was comfortable, but she was quiet and pensive, as though wrestling with some inner demon. After the movie, instead of taking her home, he drove to the observatory at Griffith Park.

"Did you bring me to make-out point?" she asked with a grin that lit up her pixie features. "I've never been up here in a BMW before."

"Oh, so you've been here before?"

"Only to the observatory," she returned with faked innocence. "What about you? You come here a lot?"

Bill chuckled. "Actually, yes. Sometimes looking at the lights clears my head. Though I usually drive up in my Blazer. It's less conspicuous than this car." He brought the BMW to a stop, but left the engine running so the music could play without exhausting the battery. Before them the bright lights of L.A. filled nearly their entire view. For long moments they stared at the display in silence.

Kylee's face was serious, and Bill hated the sorrow he saw there.

"What's wrong, Kylee? You've hardly said a word since we talked about your ex-husband. Or am I missing something?"

Kylee stared at her hands. "No, you're exactly right. It is about my ex-husband. I'm sorry. I guess . . . well, I haven't been fully honest with you, and I don't know if I can be. It's just . . . there are so many memories that I prefer not to . . ."

Bill sat up straighter. This sounded serious. What was Kylee hiding? Was it something about Nicole? No, she had said it concerned her ex-husband.

"Whatever it is, you can tell me," he said. "Or not, if you want. But you showed me last week that talking about it helps. I'd like to return the favor."

She fumbled in her small purse, fashioned of the same glittery bronze and gold that made up her dress. In her wallet she found a small photograph of Emily, the baby in the picture at her house. She didn't look at him, but at the baby as she spoke, her voice sad and far away. "It's Emily. I told you she died, but what I didn't tell you is that she was mine."

Bill didn't bother to hide his surprise. "You had a baby? What happened?"

"Well, after I left France I went to England for a couple of months and then to Morocco. It was there I met Raymond. He was on a photo shoot for one magazine or another, and in between his picture-taking we fell in love. Or so I thought. We were married in less than a month. We just took the ferry to Gibraltar. Since you're French I'm sure you've heard that anyone can get married there. Sort of a European Las Vegas. Anyway, we finished our work the next month and returned to America. It was there I discovered I was pregnant. We were both so excited, until we were told there was a very strong possibility of her having Down syndrome. All the tests pointed to it. I was five months pregnant at the time. Raymond wanted me to abort, but I couldn't." Kylee looked up at Bill now, tears in her eyes. "I knew she lived. I could feel her inside, moving. She trusted me to take care of her until she could breathe on her own. Besides, there was always the chance that the doctors were wrong." Her gaze shifted back to the photo and her voice hardened. "That's when Raymond left. He wasn't about to waste his life taking care of a disabled child.

My family tried to be as supportive as they could, living so far away in Minnesota, but I knew they agreed with Raymond that I should abort her. So I muddled through alone."

No wonder she hadn't thought to contact Nicole, Bill thought. *And what a terrible thing to suffer alone!* "I'm so sorry," he said. Of all the words offered after Nicole's death, these had held the most comfort.

"Thank you." Kylee held his gaze. "You know, sometimes I even doubted my own decision, but when she was born and they put her in my arms, I knew I had chosen the right thing. She was four weeks early and so tiny and beautiful. I loved her immediately."

Bill waited for more. *What had happened to Emily?*

Kylee swallowed hard. "It wasn't until the next day that they told me Emily had something wrong with her heart that they hadn't detected before she was born. If they had, there would have been some chance of a transplant or something, but she was already weak, and with her defect she was never really considered a candidate for expensive heart surgery. To their credit, they did everything they could. But she died the next week. I was holding her."

Tears streamed down Kylee's face as she sobbed quietly. Bill blinked back his own tears and pulled her as close as he could in the car, holding her and stroking her hair. "I'm glad you told me." He wished he could comfort her, to take away her pain. But who could make up for the neglect of a husband? Or for the loss of a child?

"I know now that it was supposed to happen," she answered, "though it took me a while to accept it. And no matter what, that week Emily and I had together was worth all the pain. My little girl is an angel, and I believe one day I'll see her again. That's enough for me."

Bill didn't contradict her. If it helped her to believe in an afterlife, then perhaps the delusion wasn't all bad. His way hadn't been easier. He still had not accepted Nicole's death, as Kylee had Emily's. For him, life was barren and bleak, often not really worth living at all. And yet now with Kylee in his arms . . .

She pulled away from him, wiping her eyes. "Goodness, it's after one! I'm not going to be awake enough to get to church, much less teach Sunday School."

Taking the hint, Bill put the car in gear and left the observatory parking lot. Only a few comments broke the silence on the twenty-minute drive to Kylee's apartment. At her door she smiled and thanked him. "I had a lot of fun."

"Well, don't forget next week. I'm still planning to uphold my end of the bargain by attending your banquet. What time should I pick you up?"

"Could you just meet me? I have to be there quite early to make sure everything's running smoothly. This is my second list I'm inviting, but I still want things to be nice."

"Your second list?"

She laughed. "Yes, as opposed to my first list. The second list is made up of wealthy people who are either not as wealthy as those on the first list, or not as generous. The dinner costs only a hundred dollars a head and the donations usually stay around a couple thousand. Other than that, it's pretty much the same. I'm even using the same catering service to serve a cut-down version of the same meal."

"You mean I could have eaten the same food for one-fifth the price?"

"Nearly. And your ten thousand would have been the top bid. They never go above that."

"Well, put me on that list, would ya? Then I can go to more dinners with you."

Kylee laughed with pleasure. "Okay, will do." She put her hand on the doorknob, but hesitated. "Guillau—Bill, I'm really sorry for sending you that invitation, addressed to Nicole like it was. You see, I was in France last month for two days on business for another charity, and I ran into your brother. Actually, it was kind of funny how we met—I've been meaning to tell you. It was at a church. I looked up the address in the phone book and went, and there he was. I didn't know he was a member of my religion until I saw him there. I was very surprised, but glad too. We were only able to talk a minute because he was headed into an important meeting. He didn't mention Nicole when he gave me your address. I guess he thought I already knew."

"You're a Mormon too?" Suddenly everything fell into place. "That makes sense. I think I sort of suspected it was something like that when I found out you had joined a church. There had to be some connection; it was unlikely you would have run into Jourdain on the streets. Anyway, it's lucky you went that day or we probably never would have met again."

"Well, goodnight."

Bill raised his hand in farewell, when what he really wanted to do was to trace her dimples with his fingers, to kiss each one before finally ending up at her mouth. He had kissed women since Nicole's death, but only because they had pushed. But Kylee wasn't pushing and he didn't want to take advantage of the emotion they had shared regarding Emily. No, it was better to let things alone.

The fact that she was a Mormon didn't bother him any more than it bothered him that his brother had joined. As long as they didn't force their beliefs on him, they should be free to do whatever they wanted.

Later, in his condo, he flipped on the TV to watch a *Star Trek* rerun. During the commercial break, the video for the Children's Hope Fund came on. Bill watched with the same fascination as when he had first seen it. The commercial wasn't the thirty-second spot he had expected, but a sixty-second one. Most likely it was cheaper to advertise at night, and so they had used the longer version of the commercial. He bet either version would bring results.

He turned to another channel, and again the tragic faces peered out at him, beckoning, pleading. All the pleas seemed to be directed at him. But what more could he do? When the burned child appeared on the screen, Bill felt a sudden rage emerge within him. He hadn't been able to help Nicole; her burned body had been beyond any earthly help. And there was no mythical God to save her, either. Or to protect these wretched children. There was only Kylee and those like her. He would give his money to their cause, but not his heart nor his hope; there might not be enough of it left to break again, but he wouldn't give anything the chance.

Bill jabbed at the remote and the room fell silent. He pulled the blanket from the other side of the couch over him, too tired to walk up the stairs to his cold bed.

That night he dreamed of the accident, of Nicole's ash-covered wedding ring glinting dully on her blackened finger. The wedding ring was the only thing that had positively identified Nicole's faceless body. He screamed, and turned his eyes heavenward, pleading, but there was no answer. When he looked down again at the woman in his arms, it wasn't Nicole but Kylee he held, her barely recognizable face turning to him, begging for help. The doctor part of him knew he might be able to save her. She wasn't burned nearly as badly as Nicole had been. The burned Kylee lifted an arm toward him, but in his dream Bill dropped her body and ran.

CHAPTER 7

Kylee was jubilant. After only seven days of TV commercials, Children's Hope had already received four million dollars more in contributions—a very good sum for the beginning week of advertising. She called Elaina with the news and then she dialed Bill at his office.

"Four million, Bill, can you believe it? In small donations from people all over the United States. And the amount should only increase because it generally takes repeat viewing for people to act. I've tried TV before and had a fair amount of success, but this time it's really working. I can't wait for the children to begin their operations! Elaina said she has them scheduled beginning next Monday. It's really going to happen!"

"Sounds like we need to celebrate," Bill said. "How about dinner? I'm finished here for the day, so I could swing 'round and pick you up."

"Oh, I don't know, our banquet isn't until tomorrow night," Kylee replied with a laugh. "Don't you think it'll ruin our record? You know, only seeing each other on Saturday banquet nights."

"Well, I think we can be adult enough to handle the conversation without having to donate money or accept awards," he said.

She giggled. "Oh, you are so funny. But seriously, I can't go tonight. That's the other reason I called. You have to watch the late news on ABC. I'm being interviewed—live! Well, almost live. They're doing a few takes and choosing the best one, but there's not going to be time for much editing. I think they're only giving me thirty seconds, plus an excerpt from my video, and a brief take of Elaina with a few children, but everyone'll see it. I'm going down to the station now."

"That means the contributions will pick up."

"I think they'll at least triple in this state," Kylee said. "And the broadcast might get picked up nationwide. I was just so excited that I had to call and tell you."

"I'm glad you did. I'm really happy for you."

"Well, you take care and I guess I'll see you tomorrow night at the banquet."

"That reminds me," Bill said. "Would you believe I actually got some business from that first banquet?"

"Well, why not? You are the best. But who was it? Someone from our table?"

There was an awkward silence. "Oh, just a lady. I really shouldn't have brought it up. I don't know why I did. Patient privacy and all that."

But Kylee was too curious to let it drop. "It was Mrs. Boswell, wasn't it? Audrey's friend. It has to be her—I saw how interested she was. What did she want? Liposuction, a facelift?"

"Well . . ."

"Come on, Bill. You have to tell me! I'm going to be running into her again, and I want to make sure I don't say anything to offend her. Besides, I think it's neat that she felt comfortable enough to go to you."

"I thought you didn't agree with casual plastic surgery."

"Well, not really, but if it makes her feel better about herself, then maybe she should do it."

"But that's just it. I don't think she has a problem with her appearance. I don't even believe she wants to do it. I think her friends are pressuring her. So I recommended a good face cream and put her on a diet and exercise program. With any luck, she won't feel the need for liposuction."

"Yuck." Kylee had seen liposuction done once on a TV program and it hadn't been pretty. "But I guess that means you really are a good doctor. I wish you could be the one to . . . Never mind. I'd better get going."

"Okay, we'll see you tomorrow."

Kylee hung up the phone, wondering again why Bill didn't want to help the children with his skills. He actually seemed to care about his patients—even the overbearing Mrs. Boswell—and had donated a lot of money to Children's Hope. That showed he cared, at least up to a point. So why didn't he want to get involved further? She shook her head and started for the door, not wanting to be late for this big opportunity.

Despite Bill's odd attitude toward doing surgery for the children, it had sure felt good to share her news with a man she could trust with her feelings. She had once felt that way about Raymond—before he had deserted her. The comparison didn't stop her budding hopes for the future. Bill wasn't Raymond and wouldn't act like him. And while she wasn't Nicole either, perhaps there would be room enough in his heart for both of them.

What bothered her most was that he claimed not to believe in God. But couldn't people change? She had. And Bill might too, given the right circumstances. Maybe she could show him the way, as someone had shown her.

She began whistling aimlessly as she slid into the seat of her car, thinking again how wonderful it was to have someone she could tell her good news.

* * * * *

Bill had heard the dial tone but he still gripped the receiver, knowing what Kylee had wanted to ask and relieved that she hadn't. He didn't want to think about becoming involved with those children any more than he already was. What if they couldn't be helped? What if their deformities couldn't be repaired to an acceptable degree? Would they look at him with reproach in their eyes, as he imagined Nicole had done while she burned in the train? He had recognized that some of the children Kylee wanted to help had diseases that were degenerative. Even with surgeries they would digress, and some would eventually die. How could he agree to be involved with something so terrifying? Hadn't he already lost too much? Better that he give sterile money and stay a safe distance away.

I'm sorry, Nicole.

He leaned his head on his fist and tried to calm his racing heart, replaying the conversation with Kylee in his mind. Her voice had been vivacious and alive, and Bill was grateful for her call—that she felt close enough to him to want to share her news. He had wanted to talk with her all week, but each time he picked up the phone, something had stopped him.

I can't help her. I can't do it.

He took a deep breath. What bothered him most was that he hadn't thought about Nicole for at least two days. As much as he had tried to forget her these past five years, that had never happened before.

He looked at the receiver still clutched in his hand and replaced it carefully. He thought again of the excitement in Kylee's voice, and how happy he had been to hear from her. She was like a slice of day in the darkness of his night.

But in all the exchange he had forgotten to tell her his own good news. Well, there was still time to get down the TV station. The address should be in the phone book.

* * * * *

When Kylee arrived at the news station, Elaina and the children were already being filmed. Anna Johnson, the youngest of the two children, clung to her mother's hand as she stared at the reporter. Anna had been adopted from Korea. She had a bilateral cleft lip, and a complete cleft palate. One of the clefts on her lip had been poorly repaired, and the other remained unaltered. Kylee also remembered hearing something about her having a temporary palate that badly needed surgery. Anna would have received it earlier, but her adopted father had died soon after her adoption and her mother didn't have the funds to pay for the necessary surgeries. They had contacted Children's Hope several years earlier and Anna had eventually worked her way to the top of the list.

"So you have a bilateral cleft palate," the reporter was saying. She spoke distinctly so that Anna could understand. The little girl had gone untreated for middle ear disease—fluid present in the middle ear at birth—and as a result suffered some hearing loss. "Anna, can you explain to us what that means?"

"I have two places on my lips that need to be fixed," she replied, her words garbled. "Right here and here." The little girl touched the thick scarred line on one side of her top lip and then the opening on the other side, both of which reached clear to her nostrils.

Anna's clefts were certainly unappealing, and because of them it was easy to overlook her beautiful eyes and her thick, shiny hair. Kylee thought how terrible it was for a child to have to deal with such disfigurement and the emotions that went with it! She had learned that otherwise Anna was like any other five-year-old girl. She craved the love and attention she was so often denied because of her birth defect.

"I also have a complete cleft palate," Anna volunteered, pointing inside her mouth.

"And what is that?"

"Well, it means I don't got a roof inside my mouth like other people, just one a doctor put there. But they say I gotta get a new one 'cause the one I got was only supposed to be there a little while."

"And Children's Hope is going to fix all these clefts?" the reporter asked.

Anna nodded.

"How do you feel about that?"

Anna glanced at Elaina with tears in her eyes. "I love them," she said. "And I'm so happy, because when they fix me I'm going to have a friend. Now no one wants to play with me." Kylee understood the words, but Anna's mother had to convey the child's meaning to the reporter.

"I'm sure you will find a friend," the reporter answered, her voice showing how touched she was by Anna's wish.

Next, the reporter turned to Jeffery Rivers, whom Kylee had first met when she had made the video. The left side of his face was badly scarred, an ear was partly missing, and one eye could only open halfway. The damage had occurred when he had been caught in the same accidental fire that had taken his parents' lives two years earlier. Now he lived with his grandfather, who loved the boy but couldn't pay for his surgery or qualify for government help.

The reporter tried to talk with Jeffery, but although he was eight, he was even more shy than Anna. For this reason, Kylee had never used him at any of the banquets, although she had believed his appearance would have been an effective motivation for the guests. Above all, the children must come first. She and Elaina had both hoped that the situation today would be less threatening for him.

"The kids tease him," his grandfather said to cover Jeffery's silence. "He's afraid."

Eventually the reporter gave up trying to elicit a response. Instead, she asked Elaina about her future plans for Children's Hope. Elaina's face shone as she explained, and Kylee was impressed with her composure and conciseness. "Our goal is to one day have enough funds so that we never have to turn away children like Anna and Jeffery," Elaina summarized at the end.

"I hope you meet that goal," the reporter replied. Then she sat back. "We've got enough, I think," she told them. "Thank you." She looked around the studio. "Is the fund-raising person here yet?"

"Yes." Kylee stepped forward. "I'm here."

"Come have a seat."

Anna left her mother and ran up to Kylee, who hugged her tightly. "I hoped I would see you," Anna said.

"Me too." Kylee hugged the little girl again. Anna's little face was filled with hope, reminding Kylee why she worked so hard.

Kylee's interview went quickly as she told about her fund-raising efforts and how people could help. When the brief interview was over, she felt disappointed that she would not be allowed to help them choose the final version of her spot, but she couldn't force them to let her stay. They knew what they were doing and she would have to trust them.

"Thanks for coming in," the station manager said to Kylee after the filming.

"Thank you for having us." She turned to leave. If she hurried, she might make it home in time to actually see the spot as it aired. She wished now that she had taken Bill up on his offer of dinner. It would have been late, but at least she would have had someone to watch the clip with. Should she go over to his condo? He had given her the code to the gate. No, he might not be home, and besides, the distance was longer to his house; she might miss the spot.

Who else could she share this triumph with? Her best friend, Suzy, attended her same ward, but she was a flight attendant and nearly always gone somewhere. Her other friends from church were younger and most likely out on dates—except for Becky who had married last year and now had a child. And of course there were many old friends that she had lost contact with over the years. She sighed. Usually she didn't miss Raymond, but tonight she did. And also Emily, who would have been nearly Anna's age by now. Kylee wondered what her life would be like if Emily were home waiting for her.

She didn't see him until he stepped in front of her in the hallway outside the studio. "Bill! What are you doing here?"

"I had to come see the taping for myself. You were good."

She laughed, all her melancholy swept away. "Thank you. I'm glad you did."

"So do you want to hang out?"

"Well, I was going home to see the spot."

"Okay. I'll meet you there." Then he added quickly, "If that's all right."

Kylee gave him a smile. "I'd like that."

When they arrived at her apartment, she hurriedly switched on the television. "Good, it looks like the news just started. They said I'd be the third or fourth story."

"Have you eaten?" he asked.

"No. I was too nervous."

"How does pizza sound?"

"Are you kidding? I love pizza. It's my favorite food." She laughed and added, "After s'mores that is."

He picked up her phone. "I seem to remember that. Mushrooms, right?"

"No, everything but mushrooms."

Bill looked deflated. "Oh, all right." He spoke into the receiver.

"Hey, it's on! Look! It's Elaina with the kids." She turned up the volume, a smile growing on her face. "Not bad. Not bad at all." Even Jeffery's refusal to speak was touching and real.

"It's great," Bill agreed, coming to stand next to her. The spot ended with Kylee's interview and a plea for help. A toll-free number for donations rolled across the screen.

"Oh, that reminds me." He pulled out his wallet. "I have a surprise for you as well. These have been arriving at my office. Apparently, many of my fellow plastic surgeons have seen your commercials and wanted to donate. Since I mentioned it at the dinner, they sent it to me to make sure it got there. I suppose they are too busy to call eight-hundred numbers."

Kylee's eyes widened as she accepted the checks. "Another miracle! It seems since we met up again my life is full of miracles." For a moment she thought she had said too much, but Bill smiled.

"For me too," he said.

They stared at each other for a long minute. Slowly their faces came closer, each watching the other carefully. Their lips met, softly at first, and then with more passion. Kylee's heart pounded in her ears and she wanted to melt into him. She had only felt this way with a few men in her life, and one had been Raymond. Everything seemed perfect.

The pizza arrived then, and they went to answer the door. A woman stood outside in the hall, her bright smile as big as the tip she hoped to receive. "How much do I owe you, uh . . ." Bill glanced at her name tag and said in a strained voice, "Nicole."

"Cole," the girl corrected. "Short for Colleen. And that'll be fifteen dollars and eighty cents."

Bill gave her a twenty. "Keep the change."

"Thanks!"

Kylee shut the door. She watched Bill, but he didn't meet her gaze as he carried the pizza to the coffee table. "Got any napkins?" he asked, opening the lid. "Pizza's good, but messy."

She touched his shoulder. "Bill?" He took his hands away from the box, finally meeting her eyes. "What just happened?" she asked.

He shrugged, his dark eyes sincere. "I don't know. I thought her tag said Nicole." He sat down and put his head in his hands. "Oh, I guess I was thinking about her. Wondering what she'd say if she knew I was kissing you. I kept telling myself that she doesn't exist anymore. She doesn't care about anything now."

Kylee sat next to him. "I think she does exist. Somewhere. But I don't think she wants either of us to be unhappy, do you?"

"If she were alive, no, she wouldn't want us to be unhappy. But she wouldn't want us to fall in the sack together either." At Kylee's reaction, Bill groaned and rubbed a hand over his face. "I didn't mean it like that. I didn't. Please forgive me. I'd better go." He arose and reached for his coat where he had laid it over the couch.

"What about the pizza?"

"Suddenly I'm not so hungry." He backed away.

Kylee sought desperately for a reason to stop him from leaving. She had the feeling that if he walked out now, she would never see him again. His guilt over losing Nicole must be deeper than she had suspected.

"Bill, wait!" He hesitated as she came to the door. "Please don't go," she pleaded. "And about what happened before, let's just forget it. I need a friend, you need a friend. I'm willing to leave it at that. Can't you stay and have a pizza with an old friend?"

He studied her face for a long moment. Then he shrugged off his coat. "Okay, let's eat."

Gradually the tension eased and they talked as though nothing had happened. Kylee found herself telling Bill about her family in Minnesota. "My Dad's a college teacher. Physics, if you believe it. For a while he was pretty sure I'd follow in his footsteps because I was always so interested in his work. But I went my own way. He was pretty disgusted when I found religion. He always taught me that man was the ultimate creation of evolution. For a long time I believed him."

"What happened?" Bill asked, taking another slice of pizza.

Kylee set down her paper plate. "Raymond left. Emily died. I finally had a reason to find out the truth for myself." She gave a small laugh. "My dad, of course, said that religion is an invention by men to answer the unanswerable, and to fool themselves into a state of false happiness."

"Well, he does have a point," Bill said dryly.

Her eyes met his. "That's what I used to think."

After a tense silence, Kylee asked, "Do you want that last piece, or can I have it?"

He grinned. "You take it—if it'll fit it in your stomach. I tell you, I've never seen anyone put away so much pizza."

"You mean a *woman* put away so much pizza, don't you?" They both laughed.

Companionably, they finished their dinner and bid goodnight. "Now don't forget the banquet tomorrow," she told him. "If you don't show up, I'm going to call Audrey and those two doctor ladies and tell them you're up for grabs." She was only half joking.

"I'll be there," Bill promised. "A deal's a deal."

And what then? Kylee wanted to ask. She was beginning to care deeply about Bill, but found it increasingly difficult to compete with

Nicole's memory. If Bill couldn't pledge his heart, then in pursuing him, she was only pursuing her own heartbreak. And a broken heart was something she didn't ever want to endure again.

For now she would give it time. But how long? When did it become too late? How long did it take to fall in love?

CHAPTER 8

Bill felt like an idiot after leaving Kylee's apartment. *What is wrong with me?* he thought. He had gone out with women in the past years, had occasionally kissed them and more, but with Kylee it was different. *Why?* Was it because she had known Nicole? Why when he had kissed Kylee did he imagine Nicole's face staring at them sadly?

For the first time in weeks he thought about his older brother in France. It would be nice to call him and talk it out, but the time difference made it early morning in France and his brother would most likely be asleep. Saturday was the only day he was able to sleep in with his family since he did some kind of work on Sundays with his church. And Bill knew from experience that by the next morning his desire to talk would have vanished. Maybe what he needed was a good workout at the gym. But it was too late tonight. Of course he could go in early tomorrow morning. Thom, a colleague, would be there. He was an experienced man in his fourth marriage, and maybe Thom would let something slip that would help. He wouldn't actually ask for Thom's advice, though, because then he would have to talk about Nicole. Bill grimaced. Maybe just pumping the iron with Thom would be enough to clear his mind.

Bill steered the BMW into his garage, thoughts of Kylee pushing everything else aside. Why had kissing Kylee reminded him of Nicole? Was it because he cared about Kylee as he hadn't any other woman since Nicole? Why should that make a difference?

He knew why, but wasn't sure he wanted to examine his feelings further. He had loved Nicole. Could he grow to love Kylee too?

And would loving Kylee demean the love he treasured for his wife? "Get over it, Bill," he told himself aloud. "Nicole is gone forever, remember? Nothing you do will change that."

Yet Kylee thought Nicole existed somewhere. With God, perhaps? Bill didn't believe that for a minute. *Jordain does,* he thought.

That was part of what bothered him. Both Kylee and Jourdain were intelligent people—how could they let themselves believe something they couldn't see? Something they could never prove?

At home, he watched TV again on the couch until his mind numbed enough to forget the pain. Then he pulled the blanket over him and slept.

* * * * *

The yellow roses were delivered at seven, a half hour before the guests were due to arrive at the banquet. The card read: *Yellow means I'm sorry.* Kylee smiled and put her face next to the roses to breathe in their aroma.

"Wow, he must have done something really bad," Elaina said with a laugh.

"No," Kylee answered. "Not really. He's a nice guy."

"Good guys are hard to come by at our age." Elaina looked over at Troy where he talked with a group of waiters. There was an unmistakable softness in her gaze.

"It looks like you and Troy are getting along well," Kylee commented.

Elaina turned to her, patting the side of her dark hair self-consciously. "Is it that obvious?"

Kylee grinned. "Kind of."

"You know, I've loved Troy for a long time. I saw him marry his wife and knew that weren't right for each other. But what could I say? That I was the one he should marry?" Elaina's blue eyes rolled expressively. "Not hardly. So I waited, I watched, I even encouraged him to stay with her when they started having problems. Sometimes it'd hurt so much seeing him with her when I knew she didn't love him like I did." Elaina looked up in the air and shook her head. "About a year ago when things got really tight at the charity, and I had to go back to work to keep it afloat, I thought about leaving. So did Troy. He and his wife had separated again, and one night we talked about quitting and letting someone else take over Children's Hope. But in the end we both stayed. I know now that it was because he loved me too, or was beginning to, and we couldn't let the charity go, or we'd be letting each other go."

Elaina sighed happily. "But now that his divorce is final we're together, and our dreams are coming true."

"Are there any wedding bells in the future?" Kylee asked.

Elaina's mouth widened in a large smile. "Yes, actually. When a little more time goes by. I've been waiting for him this long. A bit more won't hurt."

"Well, I'm happy for you," Kylee said. "And it looks as though everything else is also going well. Did you see the news spot last night? Anna was sure excited about getting her first surgery on Monday. I think she did a great job talking to the reporter. I made a few copies of the tape. I'd like to give her a copy."

"That's a great idea." Elaina paused. "But the surgery isn't going to happen on Monday."

Kylee was surprised. "What? But I thought—"

"The plastic surgeon called this morning to reschedule. Apparently, he's had some very high-paying jobs that came up and he has to take them to make up for the time he's donating to Anna. So Anna will get her surgery the first day of December. It's actually perfect timing. I mean, what a great Christmas present!"

"Yeah," Kylee agreed, but she felt slightly discouraged. "What about the other four children you had scheduled? They're not all being done by the same doctor."

"No, but they've been rescheduled too. Someone from *60 Minutes* called me and wants to follow the story. That's big. We just can't pass up the opportunity for the exposure. Now don't look so sad, Kylee. Two or three weeks aren't going to make a difference in the rest of their lives. They'll get the help the need. You'll see to that."

Kylee grinned sheepishly. "We both will. I guess I'm not very patient."

"Well, remember it's a virtue. Oh, look, Troy's calling me." Elaina gave her a wink and left.

Bill showed up with the first guests. "Thank you for the flowers," she told him.

"You're welcome. I was kind of an idiot last night. I'm sorry."

"Apology accepted. But I meant what I said. I need a friend more than I do a broken heart right now." That much, at least, was true. But what if she could have a friend who was also the love of her life?

He chuckled. "I'm sure you have friends."

"Yeah. Well my best one is a stewardess who called me this morning from Atlanta to tell me she's dating this really hot pilot, and my other best one just had her first baby. They're rather wrapped up in other things right now."

"Well, I'm here at least. Do you have a table I should wait at? Or do you have something else you need?"

"Want to greet people?" she asked.

"Not a chance."

She grinned. "I didn't think so. But our table is right over there, by the door to the kitchen. You see it, don't you? It's the one with the gorgeous yellow roses." She glanced at the growing crowd of people. "Do you think you can find your way over there yourself?"

He threw her an amused look. "If I really tried."

"Hey, Bill," Kylee called, stopping him. "You're walking funny. What happened?"

"Oh, I went to the gym this morning and had a good workout."

"Did something fall on your legs?"

"No, I'm just a little stiff. It's been a while since I've visited the gym."

Kylee struggled to keep a straight face. "Oh, I see." She put her hand over her mouth, but the laughter bubbled through. Bill grinned with her.

He waved her back to the guests. "Go on and take care of them. I'll talk to you later."

For Kylee, the greeting stage of the evening had never taken so long. She glanced often at Bill, sitting alone at his table. Once he put one of the yellow roses between his teeth and positioned his arms as though he were dancing. Kylee laughed and wondered if he liked to dance. Her church was sponsoring their monthly singles' dance in two weeks to celebrate Thanksgiving. That would be so much better than going to the smoke and booze filled dance halls. Maybe Bill would go with her.

* * * * *

When Kylee arrived at the table, Bill was telling the two couples who had joined him the details involved in a facelift. The lady next to Bill turned a pale shade of green. "Why, I would never submit to that," she said daintily. Her apparently much older husband patted her hand.

"Oh, no?" Bill said. "Hmm. That's interesting. I guess it's lucky for me that many people don't feel that way." He recognized the tiny, almost imperceptible marks on her face that most people would never see. Coupled with her older-looking hands, Bill judged that the woman had not only had plastic surgery once, but possibly twice.

The evening played out much as the benefit dinner two weeks before, and Bill noticed the donations were more generous than Kylee said was customary for her second list. The commercials, it seemed, were doing their job.

After the guests left, Kylee sat at the table with Bill, watching the waiters clean up around them. "I'm glad it's over," she confessed. "You know, I still get butterflies in my stomach when I first get up. It's okay after I start talking, but before that I'm a wreck."

"It doesn't show."

"That's good." As she spoke, she watched Elaina and Troy talking by the outside door, heads close together.

"Is something wrong?" Bill asked. "You seem kind of far away."

Kylee turned her gaze back to him. "Oh, I'm just disappointed. Remember when I told you that the surgeries were to be scheduled on Monday? Well, apparently they've been delayed. One of the surgeons had to reschedule, and then *60 Minutes* wanted some time to follow the stories of all the children, so that delayed the rest of the surgeries as well."

"*60 Minutes* will get you some great publicity."

"I know, but I just wanted to see the children get help now. Little Anna is going to look so great once her mouth is fixed."

"A bilateral cleft lip and complete cleft palate will require more than one surgery, you know." Bill said. "With a case as severe as hers, she'll need to have further surgery as she matures. That's not even including the hearing, breathing, and dental problems she has. And overall there will be a lot more scarring than if she'd had the lip surgery as a baby."

"Yes, I know all that, but she'll look good. I know she will. Certainly a lot better than she does now. We already have a great dentist, Gerald Torgeson, who's volunteered to help with the dental work. And I'm sure other doctors will step forward to help in the other areas. I hate this delay."

Bill grabbed her arm. "Come on, what you need is to get away from this for a while." He stood, pulling her up with him.

"Do you like to dance?" Kylee asked suddenly.

He gave her a pained expression. "Tonight?"

She grinned, and the dimples on her cheeks looked more alluring to him than ever. "Even I can see that you can barely walk tonight, much less dance. But we'll be having a dance at our church in a few weeks. It's being held on the Friday after Thanksgiving."

"With preaching and baptism in the intermission?" he said with a smirk.

Kylee punched the sore muscles in his arm, laughing as Bill winced. "Something like that. And of course we always have to smuggle in rock music, and there'll be chaperones. We'll have to dance an arm's length apart."

"What! But we're over thirty!"

"And while the chaperones are measuring the distance between us with hard little rulers, and frisking us for rock music, we can talk about a bridge in San Francisco that I've been meaning to sell you." She rolled her eyes. "It'll make an excellent investment—right after a tract of swamp land in Florida."

Bill laughed. "Boy, I bought into that one, didn't I? Okay, I'll go. But no bridge, all right?"

"Deal."

"So what should we do now?" He had wanted to help get her mind off the charity and surgery delays, but he didn't know where to go this late. If it were summer, he would take her down to the beach and they could stroll along the shore and . . . Maybe it was just as well it was winter and colder than normal for November.

"I play a pretty mean *Yahtzee,*" Kylee suggested. "And *Rummikub* is fun."

Bill smiled. "Why not? It's about all the activity my muscles can stand."

"I'll even roll the dice for you," Kylee said in amusement. "Boy, you really have to start exercising more."

"And I suppose you exercise."

"Nope," she admitted. "I'm allergic."

They drove to Kylee's house in separate cars as they had done the previous evening. For two hours they talked and played games, sipping soda pop Kylee had in the refrigerator and munching cashews from a can Bill kept in his car. Bill noticed that she maintained a comfortable distance between them and part of him was glad. The other part of him was frustrated by the situation, and he fought the strong urge to take her in his arms.

It wasn't until he had bid Kylee a friendly farewell and was driving home that memories of Nicole returned to haunt him.

CHAPTER 9

A week crept slowly past, bringing in another six million dollars from around the country. Public officials and celebrities joined in the frenzy, and even more money poured into the coffers at Children's Hope. Kylee kept busy with media reports, public appearances, and tracking the growing funds. She went to dinner twice with Bill, but each time their conversation was deliberately light and the distance between them marked with invisible lines.

"Sometimes I just want to hit him," Kylee confessed to her friend Suzy in frustration.

"Oh, but how romantic!" Suzy said, looking thinner than normal in her form-fitting flight uniform. She had just come from the airport, stopping at Kylee's on the way to her own apartment. "A man tragically affected by his beloved wife's death, fights to hold on to her memories in the face of his growing love for her best friend. Wow, that's good. I should be a novelist."

"Would you give it a break? I don't know how much more of this I can take. I'm really falling for him."

Suzy's smile faded. She put her arms around Kylee, her long blonde hair swinging behind her. "You be careful. I don't want to ever see you as down as you were when I met you. No man is worth that."

"I'll be careful," Kylee promised. She had met Suzy on the flight home to visit her parents after Emily's death. It was Suzy who had shared the gospel of Jesus Christ with Kylee for the first time, and that precious glimpse of eternity had given Kylee the will to survive. "But Bill isn't like Raymond," she insisted. Of course, he didn't believe in God, but Kylee knew he could change if he only felt the

Lord's love as she had. He was honest and good and kind—all important qualities for a good Christian man.

"I know he's not like Raymond," Suzy said, her ever-ready smile back in place. "But he's still a man. And that means he starts out with one strike against him." She rolled her eyes and sighed.

Kylee hugged her. "I'm glad you stopped by."

"Well, I wish I could stay longer, but I'm on another flight tomorrow to Seattle. And I can't miss it. Guess who's the pilot? Yep, Mauro. We're going to have dinner after the flight with my parents. And since I can't stay in Seattle for Christmas, I'm staying there for my week of down time. They're letting Mauro stay the night in my brother's room. Imagine that! But we'll see you when I get home."

"You're taking him to meet your parents? Then it's getting serious."

Suzy grabbed her hands excitedly. "Oh, I hope so. I hope and pray. He's great! I can't wait for you to meet him. But I really have to go now. Don't worry about Bill. Things have a way of working out. Remember, only the Lord sees the big picture. Bye now." She kissed Kylee's cheek and was gone.

By Wednesday of the following week, the day before Thanksgiving, another nine million dollars had filtered in, less expenses. Kylee was more than pleased. She made a trip to the bank, then stopped in at the Children's Hope offices in downtown L.A.

Elaina accepted the deposit slip and shook her head. "It's so much money," she said, tucking a strand of her short dark hair behind her ears. "Much more than I ever imagined raising in so few months."

"And this is only the beginning, Elaina. I can feel it. As the ball gets rolling we'll bring in much, much more."

Elaina let the bank slip drop to her desk. "There is another side to this, Kylee."

The seriousness in her voice brought a cold feeling to the pit of Kylee's stomach. "What?"

"Do you know that we've had another hundred children referred to Children's Hope in just the past few days? I can't keep up with the submissions. Many are from poor countries; they're simply grasping at any chance for a better life. I never dreamed there could be so many children out there with so many needs." Tears glistened in Elaina's blue eyes. Her hands curled into fists and then uncurled again. "I thought I could make a difference, really change something. But there is always one more child to help, one more person in pain. Sometimes I don't know if I have the strength to face it. And that's when I think about quitting and going back to a normal life. It's so much work, and I'm tired."

"I know it seems pretty hopeless when you look at all the children left to help," Kylee answered. "That used to bother me too. And some days are just plain overwhelming. But I find if I take one or two steps—in your case one or two children—and see their joy and how you've made a difference in their lives, you'll find the strength to go on. You know that, you've done it before. Elaina this is big. I can feel it! You're making the difference. And like I said, this is only the beginning."

Elaina looked at her wearily. "You're the one who makes the difference. You're the one who has changed my life. And Troy's. We'll never be able to thank you enough."

"You don't need to," Kylee impulsively touched Elaina's arm. "Well, I've got an interview with *60 Minutes* in a few minutes, so I have to be going."

"Break a leg." Elaina glanced again at the bank deposit slip in front of her. "Oh Kylee, wait. Tell me, are these funds up to date?"

"Yes. There'll be more in a few days. When it starts to peter out, we'll cut back on the commercials. But as long as they're generating profit, I think we need to keep them on."

"I'll leave that in your hands."

Kylee smiled. "I won't let you down." She took a few steps toward the door. "Oh, that reminds me. Do you have a final time on Anna's surgery? The people at *60 Minutes* wanted to know what time to have the camera crew there on Wednesday."

"Oh, then you haven't heard!" Elaina said.

Kylee didn't like the sound of that. She walked back to Elaina's desk. "Heard what?"

"Dr. Nelson had to reschedule again. But this time, for sure, the surgery will be two weeks from today, December eighth. He had only one other appointment that day to work around, so I'm assuming it'll be sometime before noon. I'll let you know the minute he confirms the exact time."

"How do we know he's not going to delay things again?"

"He won't. Not with *60 Minutes* involved. He'll get too much publicity out of this. His business will probably double. I told him that if he delayed one more time we'd get someone else."

Kylee moaned. "That means I'm going to have to reschedule everything with *60 Minutes*. I hope they won't drop us altogether."

"They won't." Elaina's voice was confident. "You'll get them to see it wasn't our fault."

Inwardly, Kylee fumed at the doctor and his constant delays. Why couldn't he squeeze Anna's surgery in? It was so odd that he would risk losing the publicity involved. Could there be something else going on?

She shrugged the fleeting thought aside. "Well at least Anna will get her surgery before Christmas."

"The others too. I have five more children scheduled for surgery the ninth and tenth."

That made Kylee feel better. "Well, Happy Thanksgiving." She made her way to the door.

"You too. I hope you plan on taking a rest tomorrow."

"I am. Bill's taking me to a restaurant that serves Thanksgiving dinner."

"Sounds fun. Maybe Troy and I'll do something like that." Elaina smiled, a soft secretive smile that Kylee envied. At least Elaina knew where she stood with Troy. With Bill, Kylee could only guess.

On her way to the hotel where the interview with *60 Minutes* was being held, Kylee refused to dwell on negative thoughts. Her life had actually changed for the better in the past few months. Her work was rewarding, and though she had been lonely with Suzy gone and Becky occupied with her baby, Bill had changed that, filling her days with companionship and affection. She looked forward to his phone calls and their outings, even just as friends.

But what if he was never ready to go beyond friendship? She didn't know what she would do. And what happened if he did decide to let their relationship grow, but still refused to acknowledge God? He seemed to be making no moves in that direction. Why was she so attracted to him? Why couldn't she walk away? She knew part of the reason was that his soul seemed to communicate with hers. He filled the parts of her that had been missing since Raymond left, and she knew she gave him back the same in return, whether or not he acknowledged it. Each day her heart waded in deeper. How soon before she lost sight of the shore?

* * * * *

Thanksgiving day dawned bright and early for Kylee. She quickly finished packing the large cardboard boxes she had begun stuffing with items the night before, and carried them to the car. Less than fifty minutes later she arrived outside Bill's gated community and punched in the code he had given her. She knocked on his door, and he opened it clad in dark blue silk pajamas.

Kylee whistled. "Nice PJs."

"Well, I knew you were coming so I dressed up." He flashed her a sleepy smile that went perfectly with his mussed hair. "Why are you here so early? I thought I was going to pick you up later to go out for Thanksgiving dinner."

"No way," Kylee said with a snort. "I decided that Thanksgiving just isn't the same in a restaurant. Now take this box into the kitchen, and I'll go back for the other one. Be careful, it has my pies."

Bill obeyed, his grin a bit dazed. For a moment, Kylee wondered if he had made other plans for the morning. *Well, he can change them,* she thought.

When she returned with the second box, Bill was waiting at the door for her. He relieved her of the burden. "Wow, what have you got in here anyway?"

"A turkey, of course. And it's about time we get it in the oven if we want to eat at one."

"At one? Dinner?"

"I always eat Thanksgiving dinner at one, don't you?"

He ran his hands through his dark hair. "Well, I never had Thanksgiving dinner before."

"Really?"

"We don't have Thanksgiving in France. And since we came here, I've tried to avoid spending time with people during the holidays."

"The women get too serious then, is that it?" she teased.

He smiled. "Yeah, something like that."

"Well, then you're in for a treat, because I'm not serious about anything on Thanksgiving except cooking. Wait until you taste my pumpkin pie. I made it last night. My apple isn't bad either."

"I can't wait."

* * * * *

Bill watched as Kylee calmly and efficiently took over his kitchen. He was still stunned that she was there, but happy to see her. Now his morning certainly wouldn't be dull, but full of life, like Kylee. She looked beautiful in her jeans and sweater that hugged all the right places. But her outfit wasn't so tight as to be conspicuous—not like the clothes some of his other dates had worn. Her short blonde hair looked clean and shiny, and he wondered if it was as soft as it appeared. He fought the urge to touch it, to take her in his arms and tell her how glad he was that she had come. *Not that road again.* He shook his head to clear the thoughts. Kylee wasn't frightening, but the growing feelings in his heart . . . *Whew! Better get out of the kitchen for a while. I could go change into some clothes. Yeah, that's it.* "Well, if I'm not needed—"

"Oh, you're needed," she assured him, pausing in unpacking the boxes. "Do you know how to make stuffing?"

"Well, no."

"Jello?"

"That I can handle." He looked down at his pajamas. "But I should change first."

Kylee's face colored, and Bill again fought the urge to hold her. *We're just friends,* he reminded himself. *You wanted it that way.*

"I'll be back in a minute." He turned on his heel and left. Once in his room, he headed directly toward the connecting bathroom. He stood under the shower for a long time, and then dressed quickly—as though afraid Kylee would have tired of waiting and disappeared.

But her dimpled face greeted him above a large bowl of cut-up bread. "I thought you'd drowned."

"I'm a good swimmer."

"You'll have to show me sometime. But right now I need to find out how to work this oven. I got the turkey in, but it seems you have to be a computer programmer to figure out how to turn it on."

"Sorry." Bill pressed a few buttons. "It's not really as complicated as it looks."

"Oh? So you got it right the first time?"

Bill grinned self-consciously. "Okay, I did have to read through the manual a few times to get the hang of it, but it does a wonderful job cooking. You can even program it to change the temperature by itself partway through."

"That would come in handy for pumpkin pie."

"How long do you want me to set it for?"

She grinned. "Until it's done. I'm not sure how long it'll take. It's a small one, though, so set it for three hours. That ought to do it."

Bill did as she asked. When he finished, she dropped boxes of orange and red gelatin into his hands, and he mixed them in separate pans as Kylee finished the stuffing. While they worked, they talked about the money coming in for Children's Hope, Bill's job, and Kylee's family. Bill couldn't remember when he had felt so relaxed and content.

"Well, that's it," Kylee said, as she poured her homemade cranberry sauce from the pan into a serving dish. "Now we just have to wait for the turkey."

"Then we'll have time to go swimming."

"Swimming?" She glanced out at the sunlit world beyond the window. "The sun is shining, but it's still rather cold for swimming. There's a breeze."

"Ah, yes, but we have an indoor pool. And a hot tub."

"But I don't have a swimming suit."

Bill was at once deflated. "Oh, yeah."

Kylee laughed. "Don't look so disappointed. I can wear a pair of your shorts and a shirt—if you really want to go."

Bill smiled, remembering the first night he had lent her his clothes. "Okay, but just don't make a habit of it. You still haven't returned my clothes from the last time."

"Oh, you're right! I completely forgot. I did wash them, and I put them in a sack—somewhere. I'll look for them tonight."

"Don't worry about it. You've been busy, and I have other clothes." He thought her consternation adorable. "In fact, keep them. Use them as pajamas or something." The idea appealed to him.

"All right, I guess. But I'm not in the habit of taking people's clothing."

"Or of staying overnight at a man's condo. It seems you're doing a lot of things lately that you don't ordinarily do. Is this a phase you're going through?"

Kylee sighed, exasperated. "Do you want to go swimming or not? Boy, you're getting to be exactly like my little brother. He never quits teasing."

"Sounds like my kind of guy." But for some reason Bill didn't like being compared to her brother.

Upstairs in his room, Bill gave her a pair of swimming trunks with a drawstring, so she could tighten them around her small waist. Then he let her pick out a thick, navy blue T-shirt from his drawer. Once dressed, the trunks went halfway to her knees and the shirt nearly covered the trunks. He handed her a huge white beach towel.

At the pool, located a short walk from the back door of Bill's condo, Kylee felt the water with her foot. "Good, it's almost warm." She threw her towel on a lounge chair and dove into the pool. The few people in the water glanced up briefly before returning to their conversations. Bill tossed the gym bag carrying their regular clothes onto the chair and followed Kylee. He tried to overtake her, but she was a strong swimmer. When he reached the far side of the pool, she was already there waiting.

"So that's why you agreed to go swimming," he said, trying to catch his breath.

She flashed him a smile. "I was our school champion, and I've gone swimming in just about every large body of water in the world. Swimming is the one exercise I'm not allergic to."

"Next time we'll try tennis."

"I can't play tennis."

"Good."

She splashed him and he splashed her back, laughing like children.

"What's this?" Kylee's soft hand traced the five inch wide scar that ran jaggedly from his shoulder down the length of his back.

"I was burned." He didn't need to add that it was on the train when Nicole had died; he saw in her eyes that she already knew. Instantly, he recalled the agony, the chilling screams, and his heart felt compressed into a small painful lump in his chest.

Suddenly, Kylee pushed him under the water, taking him by surprise. Then she swam off again, and he followed, spluttering water. Kylee's laugh echoed over the water at his futile attempt to overtake her. The death grip on Bill's heart lessened, and he silently thanked Kylee for the distraction.

When they tired of swimming they went to soak in the steaming water of the hot tub. Kylee leaned her head back. "Ah, this feels good."

It did. The heat seeped into Bill's body and made him relax. "I never want to get back in the pool after being in here."

"Why not? The change in temperature gets your heart beating. Makes you feel alive. Come on, try it." She pulled him out of the tub and into the pool. Bill gasped as the comparatively cool water enveloped his body. Before he could fully adjust, Kylee said, "Now the hot tub again." Once more he followed her, this time wincing at the heat.

"You know, I'm a doctor and I don't think this is really good for your body," he feebly protested.

"Probably not," she agreed. "But you feel alive, don't you? Tingly?"

Now that she mentioned it, he did feel vitally alive. "Yeah, I'm tingling all over."

"In high school we used to go up to these hills where there was a natural hot spring near a cold river. We especially liked to go there in the winter. We'd go into the hot water and then into the cold river water and back again. Mmmm, delicious!"

Bill noticed that the other occupants in the pool had departed, and they were alone. Kylee sat very close to him, close enough for him to hear her soft breathing above the bubbling of the hot water. So close that her leg touched his. Her borrowed shirt hung about her without defining any curves, yet he felt more attracted to her than he ever remembered. He stared into her eyes for a long moment, saw her become aware of her effect on him. She didn't move away, but sat waiting, her eyes locked on his. It would be so easy to follow his emotions, to sweep her into his arms. And yet he couldn't.

Nicole!

He eased away from Kylee under the pretense of adjusting the air stream in the tub.

"We'd better change and get back to the house," she said. "I need to check the turkey." He felt more than saw her slip out of the water.

Good, he thought. *Let's not talk about it. Then we can pretend we're still just friends.* What he didn't admit to himself, at least not in words, was how much he had come to depend upon her in the last month. How even when he wasn't with her, thoughts of her filled his mind.

She stopped and squatted down near where he still sat in the hot tub, her clothes dripping water onto the decorative cement. "Nicole would want us to be happy. I hope you'll think about that."

Before he could reply she was at the side of the pool, vigorously drying herself with the white towel before heading to the small changing room.

Bill watched her leave, feeling a numbness spread through his body. He wanted to shout for her to come back, to cry out the pain of his past in her arms, but that meant he would have to offer her something more than friendship. Why couldn't he do that? *I want to,* he thought. Maybe that was the first step—the desire to change. She was right about one thing: Nicole had always wanted his happiness.

Abruptly, he envisioned Nicole standing at the airport in Paris. Her face was somber, and tears pooled in her dark eyes. "Don't cry," he had murmured.

"I can't pretend I'm not going to miss you."

"It won't be forever. A few more months and I'll be home for good."

She sighed and gave him a weak smile. "I know. And I'm okay with that. Really. I love you . . . so much. The important thing to me is that you're happy."

He had held her then and kissed her, wishing more than anything that he didn't feel obligated to return to America and his studies. Six months later he had finished and had come home to ask her to marry him. She said yes. A month more and she was dead.

So much wasted time!

Bill shut his eyes and let himself sink under the hot water, hiding the tears that wet his face. He emerged, gasping for breath. Then he pulled himself out of the water, banishing all thoughts and feelings until he could examine them later—when Kylee had gone home.

Back at Bill's place, they went about the meal preparations with no further incident. Once more, he relaxed and enjoyed her presence. She maintained a physical distance between them, but that only reassured him there would be no more awkwardness. He didn't think he could handle another vision of Nicole or the turbulent emotions that accompanied each flashback.

When the table was set, Kylee asked if she could offer a prayer over the food, and Bill acquiesced without comment. She closed her eyes, bowed her head, and folded her arms, but he sat without moving and watched her as she prayed. Afterwards, Kylee said, "While I was growing up, my family didn't go to church or pray or anything, but at Thanksgiving we did tell each other what we were thankful for. And this time, Bill, I'm thankful that we met again. I'm thankful for your friendship. And I hope that we . . ." She paused, as though not knowing how to continue. "And I hope that it's a long one. A long friendship, I mean."

This was a custom Bill felt comfortable with. "I'm also grateful for you," he said with sincerity. "And I'm really glad you came today."

They finished the best meal Bill had eaten since he left France. Neither the expensive banquets he had attended, nor his favorite restaurant could compare to Kylee's food. Or her company.

Later, after the clean up, they whipped cream and had barely sat down to eat Kylee's pies when the doorbell rang. "More lady admirers?" Kylee teased.

"Not hardly. I've scared them off by now." Bill opened the door to his elderly neighbors, Mr. and Mrs. Simpton, both as thin as they were energetic.

"Hello Dr. Dubrey," said Mrs. Simpton. She caught sight of Kylee behind him. "Oh, we didn't realize you had company. I just made some of my turkey-shaped cookies and wanted to bring you some."

"You didn't have to do that," Bill said. The woman had taken to baking him goodies several years ago when she realized he stayed home alone for every holiday. "But I do love your cookies."

"I like to make them for you." The lady's sharp, questioning eyes were on Kylee.

"Well, come on in for a minute and meet my friend Kylee." Bill made the introductions.

Kylee smiled. "We were just going to have some pie in the dining room. Will you join us? We have plenty."

"Sure," Mrs. Simpton said. "We'd love to." Her eager eyes reminded Bill that he had never invited the couple past his entryway before.

Kylee served their guests. "This is great pie, young lady," Mr. Simpton told her. "Just like my wife's."

"Thank you."

They ate slowly, enjoying each bite. Bill had a second helping while Mrs. Simpton passed on the local gossip.

At last Kylee glanced at her watch. "I'd better get home. I've been here all day, and I've neglected a few things I just have to get done before tomorrow. Work, you know."

"But it's a holiday," protested Mrs. Simpton.

"So it is, but I really have to get going." Kylee looked at Bill as she spoke. As clearly as if she had confessed her motives, he knew she was purposely leaving while the Simptons were present to avoid any tension between them. Bill felt relief, but also a sharp disappointment.

"Well, it was so nice to meet you, dear," said Mrs. Simpton. "Dr. Dubrey doesn't have many visitors."

Bill came to his feet. "Let me walk you to the car, Kylee." He hoped that would hint to the older couple to leave.

"Well, I do have the boxes to take back with me."

"I'll help," Bill offered.

A short time later, he swallowed his annoyance as the Simptons trailed them to Kylee's car. But Kylee winked at him, dimples deepening. "See you tomorrow night for the dance. Be sure to bring your Bible." Swiftly, she kissed him on the cheek and was gone.

Mrs. Simpton patted his arm as he stared after the car. "That's a nice girl you have there, Dr. Dubrey. And it's high time you got married. You're not getting any younger, you know."

"He said they're just friends," Mr. Simpton reminded her.

Mrs. Simpton sniffed. "Didn't you hear her tell him to bring a Bible? That's more than friendship."

Bill sighed. What was wrong with him? Kylee was vivacious, beautiful, and funny—and she liked him. Even Mrs. Simpton could see that. He remembered vividly how alive Kylee had made him feel in the hot tub, and how he yearned to hold her. Nicole was dead and gone forever. Maybe it was time to stop living in the past.

CHAPTER 10

Late Friday afternoon, Kylee's world crashed. She had tried calling Elaina all day to verify the time when Anna would meet with the *60 Minutes* reporter and camera crew before her scheduled surgery. Finally she decided to go to the Children's Hope's rented headquarters in downtown L.A. The receptionist they had hired from the temp service greeted her.

"Hi, Julie. Did Elaina ever come in?" Kylee asked. "I really need to know what time the camera crew is supposed to be there on the eighth. They have to know today."

Julie shook her head. "I'm sorry. Ms. Rinehart hasn't come in so I couldn't ask her. Mr. Stutts either. They didn't come in yesterday because of Thanksgiving, but today I expected them both by nine. I've already canceled a score of appointments for them. I don't know what to do."

Kylee's irritation turned to worry. She knew they had both quit their other jobs when Children's Hope had begun to receive funds, their hands full with the new demands of the charity, and it wasn't like either of them to desert their desks. Had they been in an accident?

"Maybe we should call the hospitals," she said slowly.

Julie bit her lip with slightly crooked front teeth. "You think so? Maybe they eloped and got married yesterday, and they're just late coming in. That would explain it."

Kylee liked Julie's explanation better, but thought it was unlikely the couple had found someone to marry them on Thanksgiving. "Well, I'm going into Elaina's office to peek at her desk planner. She must have found out the surgery time by now and forgotten to tell me."

"I don't know," Julie said, hesitating.

"Don't worry, Julie. If Elaina doesn't like me going in there, I'll take responsibility."

"Would you?" Julie's face was both eager and apologetic. "Because I'm really hoping this'll become permanent. I like working here."

Kylee opened the door to Elaina's office, almost expecting it to be locked. Who would leave their office open for two days? A woman in love? Another more unpleasant thought came, but Kylee pushed it aside. She stared at the desk where only two days before Elaina had sat voicing her concerns about the additional children asking for help. Now the chair was empty. On the desk, two stacks of papers sat neatly on each side and between the stacks a single sheet of stationery lay on the desk. The note was addressed to her. Kylee read it first with disbelief and then with utter despair.

Dear Kylee,

I know you're going to hate me for this, but I can't stand the pressure. In all the years we've struggled here, I've never touched a penny, but now I'm going to find my own happiness. I can't change the world, but I can get away from it. Don't try to find us, you won't be able to. I hope you understand; it's a once-in-a-lifetime opportunity. I know the children will be all right. You'll see to that.

Elaina

A once-in-a-life-time opportunity. The words reverberated in Kylee's mind. *Opportunity? Stealing happiness from innocent children, an opportunity?* Kylee's breath came in violent gasps. In an instant, she was transported back to the day Raymond had left her.

"It's your fault," he had said, pointing at her stomach. "You're choosing that baby over us. It's as simple as that."

Was Elaina's betrayal also her fault? "You'll see to the children," she had written. Elaina knew how important the project was to Kylee. She had seen the "opportunity" and taken it, knowing that Kylee would be there to fix things.

Kylee slumped to the chair by the desk, her breath still coming ragged and harsh.

"What's wrong?" Julie appeared in the doorway, her hazel eyes wide. "You're not having a heart attack, are you? Should I call 911?"

Kylee shook her head and thrust the paper at her.

Julie read the note. "Oh, no! Does this mean she took the money? All of it? It can't be! What about the children?"

Kylee forced herself to stop crying. *Take deep breaths,* she told herself. "We don't know how much they took yet. But we'd better call the police."

"Mr. Stutts is gone too? Well, then I bet they did elope."

"Yeah." Kylee reached for the phone. "I guess they did."

The next few hours were a nightmare for Kylee. The police questioned her and checked the bank accounts held by Children's Hope. The results led them to call in the FBI.

"Apparently they had a total of about 24.6 million dollars from three separate accounts transferred to a bank in Switzerland, where it then was transferred to a series of European banks. And there we lost the trail. My guess is they're in Brazil or someplace, sipping martinis on a beach." The FBI special agent looked at her kindly. "That's all we can tell you right now. Of course, we'll probably have more questions for you later, but why don't you go home? We'll let you know when we have anything more."

Julie walked out with her to the car. "I guess that means I don't have a job anymore. Isn't there any money left at all? Poor little Anna. She was so excited about the operation. She said to me yesterday that she was sure it would bring her a few friends."

"Well, there's still money coming in," Kylee said. "But once the press gets wind of this, that'll stop. I don't know if we'll have enough to help any children."

Julie sighed. "This is so lousy. I'm really sorry."

Kylee drove home in a daze. Once there, she took out her personal bank statements and stared at the numbers without recognition. How could she help Anna and the rest? It was an impossibility. There was only one way the surgeries could go through as planned.

Bill.

* * * * *

When Bill knocked on Kylee's door Friday night, he didn't expect to find her unready for the dance. "What's up?" he asked. Her eyes were red and puffy as though she had been crying for a long time.

She stared at him, and he saw the devastation in her face. "Elaina and Troy," she began slowly. "They ran away with all the money I raised for Children's Hope. Everything except what I haven't collected in the past two days from the phone solicitation agency. Every dime." She began to cry. "I've never worked so hard in my life or achieved such success. And they ran off with everything."

He hugged her. "Oh, Kylee, I'm so sorry. When did it happen?"

She told him, looking sad and lost. "I should have known," she ended with a sigh. She walked over to the couch but didn't sit down. He followed her.

"You couldn't have known."

"But I *am* responsible." Her tear-filled eyes searched his, begging for another explanation. "I looked at their books. They were scrupulously honest. In all the years Elaina and Troy dedicated to the charity, they took payments only for their hourly work, and very modest at that. You should've seen the expense accounts of some of the other charities I've helped—exorbitant lunches, posh furniture, and weekends out of town that all came from the budget. Even clothing and gifts. Incredible. That was what so impressed me about Children's Hope. I wanted them to have the money because I knew they'd use it to do good and not waste it on frivolous things. The people on my lists trust me to do the research, to make sure their money gets where they intended it to go. I failed them all."

"It's not your fault." Bill patted her back ineffectually.

"Yes it is. Don't you see? All these years Elaina and Troy struggled and kept at it because they knew they were the only ones to help these children, and then here I come and raise more money in a few months than they raised in the entire five years they've operated the charity."

"So they ran away because you could raise money better than they could?" Bill didn't think Kylee was making sense. It must be the shock.

"No! It was because I cared!" Her eyes flashed angrily. "Because I cared, those idiots knew I'd continue to help the children once they took off with the loot." Her face became pleading. "And I have to do it, Bill. I promised Anna and the others." Kylee looked away from him, and her voice came from far away. "But how? Once this hits the papers the donations will stop. Everything will be lost. No one will trust my name again." She paused. "That's okay, my name's not as important as the children. I can change my name."

Bill blinked in surprise. "You'd change your name?"

Her gaze shifted to meet his again, challenging. "If that's what it takes! You did."

"But it can't be all gone," he insisted. "They left two days ago, didn't they? More money must have come in since then."

Kylee nodded. "There might be enough to pay for Anna's first surgery."

"See, there's a start."

She shook her head violently. "No, no, no! What about the others? There are *hundreds* of them. Hundreds! Many don't even live in America. They'll need plane fare, or we'll have to send the doctors to them. . ."

"I have some money," Bill said, wanting desperately to ease the pain in her eyes. "I have a lot of it put away. You can have it. All of it. And I'll help you get more. But you have to realize that none of this is your fault. You have to snap out of this." Bill knew his last words were harsh, but Kylee seemed on the verge of a nervous breakdown.

The frantic look left Kylee's eyes. She studied him for a long time before speaking. "You're right," she said calmly. "I do need to think about this rationally. But I don't need your money, Bill. Well, I do, but no one person has enough money to replace what Troy and Elaina stole. No one who'll give it to me, that is. There's only one thing that will let those children get their surgeries on their scheduled days and that's if you'll do them. The parts you're qualified to do, anyway."

Bill felt as though she had punched him in the stomach with a fifty-pound weight. Nicole's face came to mind, slowly blackening as it must have in the fire—when he had been too concerned over his own pain to help her. "No."

Her hands tightened into fists. "Why?" she demanded. "This is the only way! Many of the other doctors have requested a fee—a substantially lowered one, but still more than I can afford after this disaster. But you could do it for nothing."

"It's not my specialty. I do mostly cosmetic surgery now."

"But you used to do a lot of the other surgeries, and I know you must have studied them in depth when you were in school here. When we talked about Anna, you knew all about what she'd need. You could help her and many of the others. You're the best—everyone says so. Why can't you use the talent God gave you to help innocent children who no one cares about? Even Elaina and Troy, the ones who were supposed to protect them, betrayed their trust. Why can't you help? Please, Bill."

He backed away from her, his heart pounding in his chest. God hadn't given him this talent, he had earned it, every step of the way. It was all he had done since Nicole . . . A memory of a burned body filled his mind. "I can't do it."

"Can't or won't?" She took a step toward him. "Tell me what it's like to feed the ego of men and women who can't face the fact that they're getting old. Is that fulfilling?"

"I do much more than that," he growled. "I change lives in my own way. I give new hope. How dare you judge what I do by your narrow standards!"

The fury in his voice found its mark and Kylee wilted to the couch. "You're right," she murmured. "I'm sorry. I really am. I have no right to judge you. I just thought that . . ." She laid her head on the arm of the sofa and sobbed.

Bill's heart felt as though it would break. He wanted more than anything to help and comfort Kylee, but he couldn't. The one thing she wanted, he couldn't give her. He was unable to help the children. He couldn't look into their eyes and promise happiness when he didn't believe such a thing really existed. Even more, he could not face failure again.

Without another word he turned and fled from the apartment, Kylee's soft sobs following into the quiet of the hallway.

* * * * *

Kylee heard the door shut softly and knew Bill was gone. Gone in her time of need, just like Raymond. "Oh, Emily!" she whispered, and cried harder now that no one was around to hear. Near midnight there were no more tears left, and Kylee went to the bathroom sink to splash her face. Then she took Tylenol for the shattering pain in her head. She stared at the mirror, hands grasping either side of the sink. *Dear Lord,* she prayed. *What now? How can I go on again?*

But even as she thought the words, she knew that she would go on. This trial was devastating, but she had gone through worse and survived. She knew the Lord loved her and would help her again. *Thy will be done.*

She went to the desk in her room and began to plan. On her computer she typed a note to the people on her charity lists, explaining the entire situation and her intent to continue to help the children.

> *. . . I am devastated by this turn of events, but I will not let the children suffer for the sins of those who pretended to help them. Know that I will do anything in my power to see that these innocent children receive the surgeries they so desperately need. I sincerely and deeply apologize for trusting your generous funds to those with their own agenda. I know that your families and companies will be blessed as though your contributions had gone to the children as you each intended. May God keep you all.*

Next, Kylee wrote a release and readied it to fax to the newspapers. Better they hear it from her in a way that might evoke sympathy rather than allow the reporters to put their own spin on the events. She e-mailed a copy of the release to the address on the card the FBI special agent had given her, asking if they objected to her releasing the information. She marked it *urgent* and prayed for a quick response. One of the agents had mentioned a new supervisor who recently came from their San Diego field office, and she prayed the man would be settled in enough to know about her case.

Leaving the computer on, Kylee fell into bed fully dressed in the green suit she had worn all day. Seemingly moments later, she was awakened by a persistent beeping. Blinking at the sunlight streaming through the curtains, she searched for the source of the sound and finally focused on her computer. She had received an e-mail from the FBI.

> *Go ahead with your release. It won't interfere with our investigation. We have also prepared a statement for the press, but it is sadly lacking the humanistic angle so it is likely they will prefer yours. I wish you the best, and for what it's worth, I'm sorry. By the way, we've taken a hat and passed it around down here, and we've raised a bit of money for the little girl's surgery. Hope it helps.*
>
> *Justin Rotua*
> *FBI Supervisory Special Agent*

Tears of gratitude filled Kylee's eyes. Maybe she couldn't help all of the children, but at least Anna would be helped, and that was a beginning. Taking a deep breath, she faxed the news release. Already, she thought of a half-dozen phone calls she needed to make, beginning with *60 Minutes*. Elaina and Troy stealing the charity's funds would be one of their biggest stories of the year, and if she told it well enough, it might even help the children.

But who would help her and Bill? Her soul yearned for him, but he had deserted her.

Like Raymond.

Why did it always come to this?

I should never have let things with Bill go so far, she thought. *I should have known better than to fall in love with an unbeliever.*

The thoughts didn't appease her need for him, but made the loss even more raw and aching. She laid her head down on the desk and wept. Shortly, she would go on with her life and begin the mountainous work before her, but for this brief moment in time she would allow herself to mourn her lost chance with Bill.

The doorbell rang and Kylee started. Could it be Bill? She prayed that it was. She blew her nose quickly and wiped under her eyes. There wouldn't be time to hide the fact that she had been crying.

The doorbell rang again as she reached the door. *Please be Bill.*

Standing uncertainly in the hall was Anna Johnson and her mother. Anna's face, streaked with tears, was nearly lost inside the too-large coat. Her mother looked pale and ill, her red eyes swollen. Kylee knew the woman didn't own a car, and must have paid a taxi to drive her—an expense she could ill afford.

Mrs. Johnson cleared her throat. "Is it true? Julie called me and told me what happened." She gazed at Kylee, pleadingly. "Please, say it's not true."

Kylee recovered instantly from her disappointment at not seeing Bill, and ushered the Johnsons into her apartment. "It's true," she said. "I wish it weren't but it is."

Mrs. Johnson pulled out a handkerchief from the pocket of her worn coat, dabbing at her face as the tears fell. She drew her hand to her chest. "Oh, my poor Anna. She's been waiting so long!" The tears became a flood, and Kylee stood helplessly, not knowing how to help her. Anna watched them, her beautiful dark eyes filling with tears.

"Come, sit." Kylee put a hand on Mrs. Johnson's arm, worried at the gray color of the woman's face and the odd way she clutched at her chest.

"I—I can't . . . I have a pain . . . Oh, Anna . . ." Mrs. Johnson collapsed, and it was all Kylee could do to prevent the woman's head from hitting against the ground.

"Mommy!" Anna rushed to her mother's side and tried to pull her to her feet.

Kylee flew to the phone, her fingers trembling as she dialed 911.

The minutes waiting for the ambulance seemed interminable. Kylee found only a very faint pulse on Mrs. Johnson's throat, and wondered if she should begin CPR. But what if she made things worse? By the time the EMTs arrived she was frantic with worry.

They gave Mrs. Johnson an injection for her heart, but the woman didn't regain consciousness. Anna patted her mother's dark hair as they prepared to take her in the ambulance. Kylee pulled her gently away. "We'll meet them there," she told Anna.

Anna looked at Kylee, her misshapen face red and scared. "Is she dying like my dad did?"

"I hope not, honey." Kylee picked up the little girl. "Come on, let's go. On the way we'll say a prayer."

She drove rapidly to the hospital as Anna cried silently in the passenger seat. Kylee's heart ached for the child and for herself. They had both lost so much.

"It's going to be all right," Kylee murmured. "It's got to be." She didn't know if she said the words for herself or for Anna.

CHAPTER 11

At the hospital they waited for news. Mrs. Johnson had suffered a heart attack, but the extent of the damage had not been determined. Kylee blamed herself, though she knew that if Mrs. Johnson had been in good shape, the shock of finding out about Elaina and Troy would not have precipitated an attack.

Anna finally fell asleep in her arms, and Kylee continued to smooth the disheveled ebony locks. What would it mean for Anna if her mother died?

Kylee remembered the last time she had held a child in the hospital. Then the child had been Emily. She had been much younger than five-year-old Anna, and even more needy. No surgery in the world would have changed the count of her chromosomes. Emily had died in Kylee's arms, but Anna would live whether or not her mother did.

I'll adopt her myself, Kylee thought. Anna wouldn't replace Emily, and Kylee couldn't replace Mrs. Johnson, but maybe they could give each other what they both craved. She thought of all the things she would do with Anna, things she had thought to do with Emily. Her load of grief lightened. It wouldn't be easy, but she would do her best for Anna—and enjoy every moment.

Hours later, the doctor came to see Kylee. "Mrs. Johnson is going to be all right."

"She is?" Kylee was surprised. She had prayed that the Lord's will be done regarding Mrs. Johnson's recovery, and had almost been sure that she would die. "That's wonderful!" She said a silent prayer of thanks before awaking Anna to tell her the good news.

Anna's smile looked peculiar with her deformed lip. "I prayed real hard like you said, Kylee."

"And the Lord answered. We are very blessed." Kylee meant what she said. Though it might take a good deal of effort on her part, she knew she could still count many blessings. Not the least of which was this little girl in her arms. An odd lump caught in her throat and Kylee admitted to herself that she wished Anna could be hers. Or another child. Her relief and thankfulness at Mrs. Johnson's recovery could not alleviate her loneliness.

Oh, Bill. Why can't you be what I know you could be if you tried?

Kylee shook her head to clear the unwanted thought from her brain. She would carry on, knowing that the Lord would have a rewarding future in store for her. The loneliness would be borne and even forgotten at times.

"We need to keep Mrs. Johnson for two or three days," the doctor said, "but since the attack was relatively minor, she'll be back on her feet shortly. We've prescribed a special diet and exercise program that should help. We may need to do surgery eventually, but we want to see how she responds to medication and diet first." He patted Anna's head. "It's actually a good thing that this happened now when someone was nearby to get her help. People have died from less severe attacks because they didn't receive care fast enough."

"It was a blessing," Anna said.

The doctor laughed. "I guess you could say that."

Kylee pondered the doctor's words as she took Anna down the hall to see her mother. If Elaina and Troy hadn't run off with the money, Mrs Johnson might not have had her heart attack until a time when she was alone with Anna. Or maybe not until years later when the problem had grown worse, perhaps killing her in minutes. Could it be that in some strange way Mrs. Johnson's life had been spared by the whole disaster?

Well, the Lord worked in mysterious ways, to be sure. With the benefit of hindsight, Kylee always appreciated spiritual growth, but sometimes she wished the road could be a little less painful.

* * * * *

During the next few days, Kylee watched as the Children's Hope scam hit the headlines and news programs. Every television station ran parts of the video Kylee had made. Almost immediately the donations from the commercials ceased, and the stations cancelled the spots altogether. Kylee had known it would happen, but her hurt was renewed all the same. Even worse, since Elaina and Troy had paid only the bare minimum in advance, the refund from the stations would scarcely cover the charity's outstanding bills—rent, utilities, receptionist's wages, and a few credit card purchases. Kylee tried to be grateful for that much.

She collected the names of the other four children who had been scheduled for surgery and one by one called the parents or guardians of the children to tell them that their surgeries would be delayed indefinitely. They were understanding, but Kylee could hear their disappointment and vowed to make it right some day.

Anna had been staying with Kylee while her mother was still in the hospital, and Kylee enjoyed the girl's company more than she cared to admit. How empty the apartment would seem when Anna returned home. Acting as even a temporary mother had kept Kylee so busy that she didn't have a great deal of time to think about Bill or the words they had exchanged. Gradually, her anger at him lessened. She hoped he would call, but he never did.

Fortunately, everything else seemed to be working in her favor. On Tuesday morning, the last day of November and almost three full days after Mrs. Johnson's heart attack, *60 Minutes* e-mailed her and agreed to film their show on Wednesday, December eighth as planned, even offering to pay part of the costs of Anna's surgery. Excitedly, Kylee took Anna and went to see her mother at the hospital to share the good news.

"The Lord has answered my prayers," Mrs. Johnson said as she hugged Anna.

The doctor was preparing to release Mrs. Johnson, so Kylee waited around to drive her and Anna to their small apartment in Pasadena. Kylee knew the way, as she had already stopped by to pick up a few outfits for Anna. After placing a call to the pastor of Mrs. Johnson's church, she left them, knowing that mother and daughter would be well cared for.

Kylee drove home, making a mental tally of all the expenses for Anna's surgery. She was determined to help at least this one little girl—even if she had to take out a loan or sell everything she owned. The *60 Minutes* show was tentatively scheduled to air the week of Christmas, which should help with donations for later surgeries. Over the past few days, people from Kylee's ward had also donated money, and with these heartfelt contributions came the bigger gift of hope.

When Kylee arrived at her silent apartment she found enough courage to look at the second name on Elaina's list of needy children. It was Jeffery Rivers—the little boy who had also been at the TV station that night with Anna.

She remembered how each time she had seen Jeffery, his burned face had cried out for assistance. *You are next,* she told him. She didn't look further down the list of children because she knew their situations would be just as compelling, and she couldn't help them all—yet. Blinking furiously, she put down the list and began to type on her keyboard. She had to get her reply to *60 Minutes* just right before she e-mailed her acceptance of their generous offer. Now that Bill had deserted her they were her only chance. If people all over America could understand how much she wanted to help the children, maybe she could regain their trust.

* * * * *

A fog encased Bill's entire existence—and had since the night he left Kylee. He sat on the sofa, staring at the blank TV and wondering why he couldn't find the strength to move. In the week since he had walked out on Kylee, he had gone through the motions of living, feeling nothing but numbness. He couldn't remember what he had eaten that morning, though he did know that he had called in sick for the third time this week, rescheduling a multitude of patient appointments, or sending them to other doctors at the Plaza, something he had never done before. What was wrong with him?

He thought of his practice and the women and men he had performed surgery on over the years. He believed he had helped them. It was true enough that some of his clientele were vain and rich, and annoyed even him, but many were simply lost souls who needed to put their lives back on the right track. He had helped women who had only one developed breast and young girls with terrible acne scars, or oversized noses that evoked taunts from cruel classmates. There had been numerous patients and he had fixed them all. Yet none of them had needed him for very long, and all could pay for their services. If he hadn't been there, they would have gone to another doctor.

Bill sighed, deep and long. So what good had he done in his life?

None. All good had died with Nicole. Since then he had been in a limbo that couldn't really be considered living. What was the use of trying? Why couldn't he just slip into the cold, welcoming grave and be done with it?

Unbidden, Kylee's face came to him. If she were with him, she would talk him out of this mood, make him feel that his life was worth living. Her laugh would banish the darkness in his mind, and her beautiful pixie features would almost make him believe in real fairies, in magic, and perhaps even miracles. But she wasn't here, and Bill didn't think she would ever want to see him again.

He stretched out on the couch and stared at the plain white of his ceiling. The agony in his heart was terrible, like on the day he had held Nicole's burned body and cried, wishing it had been him instead. The only light on that day had been the loving embrace of young Pauline. How wonderful she had felt in his arms when she had hugged him, alive and vital. She reminded him of the child Nicole had once been. Now both were dead. What terrible unfairness!

Bill cried. He didn't sob or make a sound, but tears cascaded down his cheeks in sheets. He felt empty and utterly alone.

For a moment, he wished there was a God as Kylee insisted. He wished he could pray and obtain some kind of comfort. He was so miserable that he didn't even smirk at the thought.

The phone rang three times before Bill realized the sound wasn't coming from his imagination. He so wanted Kylee to call, to hear her voice. To ask for her forgiveness without giving anything in return. But deep inside he knew she wouldn't call. He had hurt her too deeply. It was one thing to refuse to give his help, but it was quite another for him to desert her in her hour of need. Why couldn't he have supported her?

He fumbled for the phone, hope battling against hope. "Hello?" His tears had ceased, but his voice sounded like gravel.

"Guillaume, it's me, Jourdain," a voice said in French. With the voice came the image of his brother—brown hair and eyes, slightly prominent nose, and sharp chin.

Bill's first impulse was to hang up. He didn't need the past intruding further into his present, or to hear how wonderful his brother's life was going since he had found religion—and a wife and kids in the bargain.

His second impulse was to cry out his problems on his older brother's shoulder.

Instead of giving in to either impulse, he schooled his voice to be calm. "Hello, Jourdain. It's good to hear from you." It had been so long since he had spoken his native French that the words came out awkwardly.

Jourdain didn't tease him about his accent as he normally did. "What's wrong?" he asked. "I can tell by your voice that something's wrong."

"I'm fine."

"No you're not."

"I'm just tired. It's still morning here."

"Not that early. By my calculations it's about eleven. Why aren't you at work?"

"I didn't feel well."

"So something *is* wrong."

Bill wanted to strangle his brother. He always had a knack for getting to the root of things. "That's why I'm tired. I'm sick." *Sick of life*, he added silently. "Why are you calling, anyway, if you knew I'd be at work?"

"I don't know. I just felt . . . Look, is everything really okay?"

Abruptly Bill's silent tears began again. *No, everything is not all right,* he wanted to scream. *Nothing has been right since Nicole died. Until Kylee . . .*

"Whoa, slow down," Jourdain said.

Bill realized he had spoken the words aloud, and a sick feeling formed in the pit of his stomach.

"Who is Kylee? Wait, do you mean that fund-raising lady you and Nicole knew? The one I gave your address to?"

Bill wanted to tell him to mind his own business, but the love in his brother's voice was unmistakable. How long had it been since they had really talked? Once they had been as close as he and Nicole. Perhaps even closer in some ways.

"Yes."

"Oh, yeah," Jourdain said. "I ran into her here a couple of months ago and gave her your address. To tell the truth, I hoped she'd look you up. Seemed like a nice girl."

"You forgot to mention Mormon."

"So? What if I did? She's still a nice girl."

Bill didn't reply.

"So I guess she looked you up, no?" Jourdain pressed.

"She did. But she didn't know about Nicole."

"Oh, no." There was deep remorse in his brother's voice. "What happened? Tell me about it."

Bill began to talk, finding to his surprise that the words came easily. He told Jourdain about the way he had gone to Kylee's benefit dinner and how they had begun to date. He explained how she made him feel. And the way he had walked out on her.

"So what are you going to do?" Jourdain asked.

Bill snorted. "Aren't you supposed to tell me?"

"I wish I knew what to say," Jourdain replied, seeming not to hear the sarcasm in Bill's voice—or perhaps ignoring it.

"I can't help her." Bill let a note of sullenness enter into the words. It made him feel better to be angry at Kylee for expecting too much from him. "That's what she wants."

"Why can't you?"

The harmless question made Bill's anger mount. "Because I can't, that's why! I won't have anything to do with it. I won't." His voice became low and desperate. "I just can't."

"Oh," Jourdain said, as though he really did understand. He was silent a minute before adding. "I remember a time when you talked about using your skills to help children. Don't you remember?"

"No." Bill's reply was short. And also a lie.

"Well, I do. You talked about it when you visited during your schooling. I remember distinctly when you told Nicole. She really liked the idea. You were full of plans. Do you really not remember?"

Bill grunted in response.

"So what happened to the idea? Why can't you help your friend now? It doesn't make sense to me, and I bet it doesn't to her either."

Bill said nothing. He thought about hanging up.

"Guillaume, are you still there?"

"Yes."

"Well, don't hang up. Please. I want to help somehow if I can. I miss you, you know. A lot. And I want you to be happy."

The plea in his brother's voice stopped Bill from breaking the connection.

Jourdain took his silence as encouragement. "I think you have to ask yourself why you turned completely to optional aesthetic surgery, Bill. Isn't that the real question?"

"I'm helping people."

"Don't be so stubborn. I'm just trying to help."

"Well, you're not."

"You know what I think?" Jourdain asked. "I think that you do what you do because you don't want to get your heart involved. I think you're afraid to care about anyone or anything because you don't want to get hurt."

"Nonsense!"

"Is it?"

Bill didn't reply. His emotions swirled around inside him, threatening to break loose.

"One thing you have to understand," Jourdain continued, "is that accepting Kylee probably means accepting those children. They are part of who she is. Now, it's obvious to me that you're in love with her, and it's not every day that you get a second chance at love. Are you going to give that up, Guillaume? Please don't. I know that the Lord has plans for you, and that He wants you to be happy."

"He's done nothing for me," Bill grated.

"Maybe you are too blind to see." Jourdain's voice was soft but firm.

Where does he get his assurance? Bill wondered. *And what about Kylee?* It was hard for him to digest that after all the devastation in her life she could still believe in God.

"I don't know who I am anymore," Bill confessed softly.

Jourdain was silent a long moment. "You're my brother and I love you."

"Thanks." Bill meant it. He didn't agree with all his brother's words, but knowing there was someone who loved him unconditionally gave him some hope.

Was there any chance at all that Kylee could feel the same unconditional love for him?

But, no, he couldn't expect her to give everything and him to give nothing.

Bill sighed. "I have to hang up now, Jourdain. I appreciate your call." Without waiting for a reply, Bill severed the connection. His stomach rumbled but he stared into nothingness.

Abruptly, an urge he hadn't felt since another lifetime came over him. He jumped to his feet and took the stairs two at a time. In the exercise room, the drawings Kylee had wanted to see that first night still lay scattered on the floor.

He flipped through the old drawings, not really knowing what he was looking for until he had found it—the drawing he had done of Kylee when he found her sleeping on Nicole's couch in France. With it came the memories of that night. Nicole had gone to the closet to hang up her coat, and he had stumbled into the living room where Kylee was sleeping. She had been so beautiful, lying in innocent abandon, untouched and untouchable; and in that instant he needed to draw her with an urgency he had never experienced before, not even with Nicole. The following week he had gone back to America and had put the incident completely from his mind.

Until now.

Bill took up his charcoal pencil and a pad and began a sketch of Kylee as she had looked in the glittering bronze and gold dress on the night of his award dinner. Had there ever been a woman more beautiful or desirable? Then he drew one of her as she had appeared later that same evening when she had told him of Emily. And still another of her glaring at him when he had refused to help the children, tears of hurt and anger in her eyes. Next he sketched one of her sobbing on the couch. He continued drawing until his hand ached and his eyes could no longer see through the tears. Then he set the pad down and stretched out on the floor, closing his eyes. Fresh anguish and loss joined the old pain he had carried with him for so long. He had again lost the woman he loved. But unlike with Nicole, he had made the choice to desert her.

He reached out to the drawings, wishing it was real flesh that his finger touched. "Oh, Kylee, what have I done?"

He began to draw again. And this time what emerged under his stiff fingers frightened him. It was Anna, the little girl from the TV station, and next to her was Jeffery, the burned child who so strongly reminded him of Nicole's death.

Bill swallowed hard. He couldn't help them, he couldn't! And he didn't want Kylee or anyone else to depend upon him—especially a burned child. There wasn't enough of his heart left to risk losing again.

Or was there?

CHAPTER 12

The days passed agonizingly slow for Kylee. She missed Bill desperately, but she didn't call him. She busied herself going over bank accounts and trying to find doctors and companies to donate time and resources. She had little success, but wouldn't let herself quit.

Finally, the long-awaited December eighth arrived. That morning Kylee met the *60 Minutes* crew at the Hubbard Craniofacial Center for Anna's surgery. Little Anna and her mother had just arrived and were talking with Dr. Nelson and several nurses. Anna's face brightened as she saw Kylee. Releasing her mother's hand, she ran to Kylee's side. "Oh, Kylee, it's finally here. I'm so excited!" Though the words were garbled and the smile twisted, her happiness radiated from her beautiful eyes. Kylee felt Anna's gladness blot out much of the pain she had been feeling. Over time this child would be able to smile without her impairment marring the effect.

Kylee bent down and hugged her. Holding the child partially filled the ache in Kylee's heart. "I'm excited too!"

"Why are you crying?" Anna asked.

Kylee wiped at her face. "Sometimes adults do that when they're happy."

Anna shook her head and pursed her lips as much as she was able with her unrepaired cleft. "That's weird. Mommy's been crying for lots of days."

Kylee knew that although she had assured Anna's mother of her continued support, Mrs. Johnson must still be worried that there wouldn't be enough funds to pay for everything. Besides the plastic surgeries and regular doctor visits, there would be dental visits, audio tests, and speech therapy. There was a long way to go, and years of medical bills. And Anna was merely the first child on the list. Suddenly Kylee's tears took on a new meaning: the costs to help the rest of the children would be staggering, and the only way she could proceed was by faith.

Feeling eyes upon her, she glanced up to see a camera turned in her direction, the red recording light burning. "Everything will be fine," she murmured to Anna. "For you and your mommy. I'm going to make sure of that . . . somehow."

"Come on now, Anna," a nurse said. "We need to prep you for surgery. Don't worry, your mom can come with you."

Anna left with her mother and the nurse to prepare for the surgery that would close her remaining cleft lip and rework the badly repaired side. The temporary palate would be replaced at a later surgery after some necessary dental work.

Dr. Nelson came up to Kylee. "I'm really sorry about everything that happened. I had no idea when Ms. Rinehart called to postpone the surgery again that she was going to do something like this. I guess I should have suspected, but I didn't."

"*She* postponed the surgery?"

"Yes. Twice."

So it hadn't been the doctor after all. That meant Elaina and Troy had been planning their escape since at least the night of the second benefit banquet. Kylee felt sick to her stomach. How could she have suspected nothing?

"Look, you won't be receiving a bill for my part in this surgery," Dr. Nelson said. "And you can count on me to help on some of the other surgeries. Of course, I'll have to charge at least minimal fees for the others to keep paying my bills. I can't help all the children you have lined up, but I can help some. I wish I were more established financially so that I could do more."

Kylee smiled at him gratefully. "You're doing what you can, Doctor. And I'm grateful. I wish there were more people like you." *I wish Bill were more like you,* she added silently. She had heard nothing from Bill since he had left her that Friday more than a week and a half earlier, and she hated to admit how much she missed him.

"Well, if you'll excuse me." The doctor nodded at her politely before turning down the hall in the direction Anna and the nurse had disappeared.

As part of *60 Minutes*' arrangement to pay some of the costs of the surgery, their camera continued to record throughout the procedure. Kylee watched on a monitor in the hall, her stomach in a tight ball as the doctor's deft hands moved confidently over Anna's sleeping face. Having met him only today for the first time, Kylee was impressed with what she saw.

But she continued to worry about money. Though Dr. Nelson had waived his fee for this surgery, the hospital bill would still apply, and she knew the charges wouldn't be low. It was a good thing *60 Minutes* had offered to sponsor part of the costs. At least Anna was on her way to full health.

One among hundreds.

Too bad she didn't have the money Elaina and Troy had taken. Then she could pay for more surgeries and not even worry about searching for a doctor to do them for free.

"This is going to make a good story," said Deedra, one of the ladies from *60 Minutes*. "As soon as Anna has recovered enough so that our viewers can see the improvement, we'll be able to air the show. Then we'll do an update when she has her next surgery."

"Thank you," Kylee replied simply.

Deedra touched her shoulder. "Don't look so dismal, Ms. Stuart. I know this has been hard for you, but when we air the show, I think public opinion will change and they'll be willing to help you rebuild. You'd be surprised at how forgiving people actually are."

Her words were comforting and Kylee felt grateful. "I hope you're right." Kylee just wished it wouldn't take so long. Thoughts of Jeffery, the second child on the list, filled her mind. How would it have been to lose your parents and go through life so terribly disfigured? Jeffery must have endured teasing and so much heartache. Impulsively, Kylee opened her mouth. "It's just that the next little boy must be so disappointed not to get his surgery. It was to have been done the same time as Anna's." Along with four others she had been forced to cancel. *Oh, Elaina what have you done?*

"So what's his story?" Deedra looked idly at the monitor, as though not completely listening.

"His parents died two years ago in a house fire. Jeffery was burned, but one of the neighbors was able to get him out. He lives with his only relative, his grandfather. They just simply can't afford the medical care he needs, yet they don't qualify for any but the basic government help."

Deedra looked away from the monitor and met Kylee's eyes. "That might make a good hook. If the people could see the child they would be helping next . . ." She let the sentence die away, her meaning clear.

Kylee nodded, stifling the rebellion in her queasy stomach. Deedra was trying to be nice, but the bottom line for her was the story; she didn't think of these children as victims but as ratings. *Did she ever wonder how many nights they or their loved ones had cried themselves to sleep?* But even as the thought came, Kylee clenched her jaw, ready to forge ahead with whatever she had to do to help Jeffery. Her pride or Deedra's intentions couldn't get in the way of saving another child. Additional images came to Kylee—nameless youngsters she had met the day she had filmed her video. What about them? The knot in her stomach crept upwards to her heart. *I can't look beyond Jeffery,* Kylee thought, *not yet.*

She gazed steadily at Deedra. "Will today work for you?"

A slight smile played on Deedra's face. "We can work it in as soon as we finish here. I'd like to do it at their home for the mood."

"I'll call and set it up." Kylee figured that if the boy was at school she could pick him up herself on the way to his home. *This has to work. It just has to.*

* * * * *

Bill pulled into a parking place and switched off the engine of his Blazer. His mouth and throat were as dry as the day he had walked three miles in the Arizona desert when his car broke down on the way to Mexico. He had been with three other medical students, and they had joked a lot about dying of thirst. But at last they had found a gas station with an attendant willing to give them water and take a look at their car.

Remembering that day brought back the rest of the trip. Hordes of little Mexican children, many not more than two years old, pushed their wares on him, eagerly grabbing his money. Some of the small faces had shocked him. Birth defects such as little Anna's, or damage caused by accidents were all too noticeable. Obviously these people didn't have the funds to help their children. It was shortly after the trip that he had signed up to study more in depth about the surgeries that would most benefit such children. Nicole, engrossed in her own obstetrical career, had been pleased. He knew that the ensuing studies had contributed to his current success as a plastic surgeon. There was nothing he could not fix; it was as though he felt in his being how the cutting should be done, how each stitch should be made.

Bill swallowed hard and carefully folded the memories away for later study. There had been so much in his life that he had put on hold, or even forgotten. The question Jourdain had asked him last week kept coming back to him, despite Bill's attempt to bury it. Why had he turned almost completely to optional surgery? Was it because those patients didn't need him? Was it because their plights didn't require his heart? Was Jourdain's assessment correct?

The idea made him more uncomfortable. His throat throbbed, and it was almost as though he tasted ashes as he had that terrible day in France. Then the ashes had been Nicole's. Whose were they now?

Better not to think about it.

He must find Kylee. The past week and a half of separation had been too long and painful. He couldn't stare at the drawings anymore, working up the courage to face her. He had to see her now, to beg her to let him have some part in her life.

Leaving the Blazer, he made his way into the Hubbard Craniofacial Center. "I'm here to see Kylee Stuart," he said at the desk. "She's with the group who is helping—"

"Little Anna," replied the dark-haired receptionist. "Yes, I know. But you're not allowed—"

"I'm a doctor too." Bill didn't often abuse the prestige of his profession, but he had to see Kylee before he lost courage altogether. Would she even want to see him? She had to! He needed her so desperately. "Dr. Dubrey."

The woman smiled, her hazel eyes suddenly bright and eager to help. "I've heard of you. Come on, I'll take you back. The people from *60 Minutes* are going to take aftershots of Anna."

It wasn't hard to find the camera crew. They were gathered in the recovery room where Anna was beginning to come out of the anaesthesia. Her upper lip was swollen almost beyond recognition, as was the skin around it, but she gave them a weak smile.

"We've got enough here," announced a woman in a striped suit. "Let's get over to the boy's house."

"Uh, excuse me," Bill said. "I'm looking for Kylee Stuart?"

"She just left," the woman told him, "but we're going to see another patient of hers right now."

"Could I have the address?"

The woman hesitated, but Anna's doctor stepped forward. "You're Bill Dubrey, aren't you?"

Bill flashed a smile he knew didn't reach his eyes. More than anything, he wanted to leave and find Kylee. "That's me," he managed.

"I thought I recognized you from that plastic surgeon's banquet." He held out his hand. "I'm Curtis Nelson. Nice set up you have there at the Plaza, with all the doctors you need in one place for helping children like Anna. That's what I hope to have here one day. Of course, I'll need a few partners. You aren't looking to relocate, are you?"

Bill chuckled politely, secretly irritated at the doctor's suggestion. *Why can't everyone leave me alone?* He knew he was being unfair, that these people couldn't possibly know of his inner turmoil and suffering. "Not at the moment," he answered shortly. "Now where did you say Kylee was? I really need to talk with her."

The lady from *60 Minutes* copied something from her planner onto a pad of paper and tore off the sheet for him. "It's the address of the next child she wants to help. We're hoping to raise funds with the show."

"I wish I could help more," Dr. Nelson said, his forehead wrinkling with concern. "But I also have to pay the bills. I'm in debt for this place up to my ears."

The woman smiled. "We do understand, Dr. Nelson. Perhaps one day Ms. Stuart will be able to raise enough money to actually be able to pay a few doctors to help these children full time." She turned to the crew. "Come on, guys. Let's get packed up. We have a time limit here."

Bill took one last look at Anna. Her mother sat by her side, smoothing the small ebony head. The hope and exhaustion in her face made Bill remember the helpless children he had seen in Mexico. His dry throat returned in force. *Where is a drinking fountain when I need one?*

As he left the room, Dr. Nelson called after him, "Let me know if you change your mind, Dr. Dubrey. With someone of your prestige, we could attract a lot of specialists. We could help more children like Anna."

Bill lifted one hand in a wave, but didn't reply. His throat was too constricted. He reached his Blazer with relief and stared at the address, recognizing its location as one of the poorest sections of L.A.

He drove faster than usual, trying not to think of what awaited him. He could do this, *he could.* He had lost Nicole, but maybe he could still have at least a small part in Kylee's life. If only he could find her before he lost his courage. He hoped she would forgive him.

CHAPTER 13

Kylee didn't think about Bill as she raced to the Rivers' home to brief Jeffery and his grandfather. Or at least she told herself she didn't. In reality, she thought a lot about him. They had spent many fun nights together, had enjoyed conversations on the phone; and now she ached to hear his voice. How happy they'd been that Thanksgiving day! *I'll probably never see him again.* The thought hurt terribly.

Mr. Rivers walked up his crumbling driveway to meet her, his barrel chest covered by a thin navy jacket. He moved with the awkward gait of the very old. It was obvious that he didn't get around very well, and Kylee wondered who played ball with Jeffery now that his dad was dead. Did anyone take him to the park?

Jeffery peered at her from behind the solid bulk of his grandfather. "Oh, you're here already," Kylee said.

"He ran home fast when I called and talked to his teacher," Mr. Rivers answered. "The school ain't more'n two blocks away."

Kylee grinned at Jeffery, hoping to draw him out of his shell. The people from *60 Minutes* would be there soon, and she didn't want him to refuse to talk as he had that night at the TV station. At least today they were on his turf, and that might make the difference. "You must be a good runner," she told the boy. "I used to like to run when I was a kid. It was fun."

As she spoke, Jeffery smiled shyly—or tried to. The left side of his face twisted awkwardly. His left eye could only partially open. "I'm the fastest runner in the third grade." His voice was soft and unsure.

"I bet you are. You'll have to show me soon. You do remember me, don't you?"

"Yeah. When we made the video and when we was on TV. I liked that." He came into full view, apparently feeling safe enough to leave the protection of his grandfather's body. "Gran'pa taped it so I watch it sometimes. I liked being at the station."

That surprised Kylee since he had been too shy to speak to the news reporter. "Well that's great! You know why? Because someone's coming over to talk with you again, and this time you'll really be on TV for a lot longer. And it'll help us raise money so that we can fix your eye and your face."

"My ear too?" he asked.

"Your ear too."

Mr. Rivers cleared his throat and said to Kylee. "Does he look all right? I don't see so well these days."

Kylee made a show of examining Jeffery. "Well, your shirt is clean, and you look like you just combed your hair."

Jeffery giggled and ducked his head. "Gran'pa did."

"Hey Jeff, do you have a ball?" Kylee asked. She glanced up to make sure there were no rain clouds in the crisp blue sky. "I bet we can play some catch before the camera guys get here—what do you say?"

His eyes widened. "Sure, I got a ball. I'll be right back. Not sure where it's at."

"Get your jacket, or a sweatshirt," she called after him. "It's a little cold out here."

He disappeared into the tiny, rundown house. Kylee zipped up her own jacket, thinking of Minnesota where she had played in snow drifts taller than her father.

"What that boy needs is a mother," Mr. Rivers said quietly. "I wouldn't give him up, not for anything, but I . . ." He trailed off, his head shaking slightly with age. "I wish he had more. I wish I could give him more."

Kylee put her arm on his shoulder. "You love him a lot. And love can make up for almost everything else."

There was a heavy silence as he fought to keep his emotions under control. "Thank you. And thank you again for helping Jeff. It means more to me than—" He broke off and wiped at his eyes with thick, weathered fingers.

She was almost relieved when a vehicle drove up behind her. She didn't have the money yet to help Jeffery, and she felt Mr. Rivers' gratitude was premature. What if in the end she couldn't help Jeffery? *Stop it,* she told herself. *Where is your confidence? You will find the money even if you have to knock on every door in this valley. You'll do it on your knees, if you have to.* Her thoughts broke off as she saw Bill spring out of a dark green Blazer. The sight of his handsome face was so comforting that for a moment she wanted to throw her arms about him.

Of course, she didn't. Why open herself to further rejection?

"What are you doing here?" she asked.

"I need to talk with you."

"How'd you find me?"

"I went to the Craniofacial Center. They said you were . . . Does it matter?" He looked pointedly at Mr. Rivers. "Can we talk?"

"I guess I could help Jeffery find the ball," Mr. Rivers said. He glanced back and forth between them with obvious relish.

Kylee laughed at his expression. "Yes, please do that."

When he had left, Bill reached for her hand. She let him take it, but kept her muscles limp and unresponsive. She felt emotionally exhausted and wondered if she could take any more surprises.

"You were right, Kylee," Bill told her. "About all of it. I know I should help, but I . . ."

Kylee stared.

"I feel bad for leaving you that day." He squeezed her hand. "I'm not what you want me to be, but I'm willing to work on it. Your . . . uh, friendship means a lot to me."

Kylee could tell the words cost him. "What do you mean, 'work on it'?" she asked, unable to suppress the budding hope within her.

Agony and indecision radiated from his face. "Kylee, I want to be here for you. I just don't know that I . . ." He stopped.

He still wasn't saying what Kylee wanted to hear, but it was enough at that moment to have him near. Oh, how she had missed him, imperfections and all! She wanted to kiss him, but thought it best not to drag up that issue again.

The *60 Minutes* van pulled up behind Bill's Blazer. "Oh, good," Kylee said. "They're here."

"For what?"

"To film Jeffery. He's the next little boy I'm going to help." She introduced Bill to the people he had previously seen at the Center.

"I found it! I found it!" Jeffery burst out of the house, wearing a worn sweatshirt and carrying a ball in a large battered baseball glove. His lopsided half-smile faded as he saw all the new people.

"We were going to play ball," Kylee explained.

"Good idea," Deedra said, straightening her jacket. "We'll film you. It'll make a great shot. And then we'll go inside and talk to them." She glanced at the small house with a frown. "I hope our equipment fits. Well, we'll make it fit. We've done it before."

To her surprise, Deedra's face showed a compassion Kylee had not suspected. *I was wrong about her,* she thought. *Deedra does care. Maybe that's why she's so willing to help. Perhaps her preoccupation with her job is just a pretense.*

As Deedra strode off purposefully to speak with her crew, Kylee turned to introduce Jeffery to Bill. "This is—is . . ." Her words stumbled as she saw how pale and drawn Bill had become. "Are you okay, Bill? You look like you need to sit down. Bill, what's wrong?"

Bill said nothing. He didn't look her way, but stood motionless, staring at Jeffery for a long silent minute. Jeffery shifted uncomfortably and glanced around, apparently searching for something. "Gran'pa?" he asked in a scared voice.

Kylee stepped over to him and put a steadying hand on his shoulder. "It's all right, Jeffery. I think Dr. Dubrey isn't feeling well. Bill, would you like me to take you to your doctor or to the hospital? You're scaring me."

* * * * *

Bill heard Kylee talking, but didn't understand what she said. He couldn't take his eyes from Jeffery. "He was burned," he said with difficulty. Burned like Nicole had been burned.

"But he can be helped." Kylee met his gaze, filled with silent pleading.

He looked away from her and back at Jeffery, who shifted nervously.

Bill had come to find Kylee to ask her to forgive him, and maybe even to offer to help her with Anna, if that was the only way she would have him. But not this burned child. Never. The only thing he saw when he looked at this boy was the train. He could hear the terrible screams.

There was nothing he could do. Why had he even come? Bill wished the earth would open and swallow him, putting an end to his misery.

Kylee didn't back down. "You couldn't help Nicole, but Jeffery here, he needs you."

How well she knew him!

Bill swallowed slowly, feeling faint, unable to do anything but stare at Jeffery and the superimposed image of Nicole. There was nowhere to run or hide, which was just as well since his legs couldn't move.

A brief cry came from the back of Jeffery's throat, a feral sound of fear and anguish. All at once Bill's vision cleared and he saw a helpless child cringing under his gaze, one thin hand held against his scarred cheek as though trying to hide his deformity.

He's just a little boy.

Compassion vied with the hurt inside Bill's heart. He fought to stem his torment so that he could do something—anything—to help Jeffery. It wasn't the child's fault he had been burned, nor that his appearance brought Bill such painful memories. Bill swallowed twice more, feeling the dryness more acutely in his throat.

Ashes.

Say something, he told himself. His heart pounded mercilessly.

He opened his mouth and was almost surprised when words actually emerged. "Hi, Jeffery. I'm Dr. Dubrey." Unsteadily, he offered his hand to the child. "I'm sorry if I startled you. You just reminded me of someone I once knew. I miss her a lot."

Jeffery relaxed slightly, and Bill's racing heart began to ease. He studied Jeffery's face, seeing that there was much he could do for the boy. His fingers tingled.

I can do this. Taking a deep breath, he said, "I'm hoping to be your doctor, if that's okay with you." *There, that wasn't so hard.* Bill blinked furiously to stop the tears welling in his eyes.

Jeffery smiled gratefully, but still appeared hesitant and uncertain.

Kylee made a glad noise, but Bill didn't dare look at her. His emotions were too close to the surface. He pointed to the tattered mitt dangling from the boy's hand. "Nice glove there. Was that your Grandpa's?"

Jeffery nodded, the scarred face turning bleak. "And my dad's when he was boy. It's mine now. It only got burned a little." He showed Bill where a dark spot marred the tan leather.

"I bet it still catches good," Bill said. "Let's try it." He held his hand out for the ball and Jeffery dropped it and took off into the deserted street, raising his gloved hand for the catch.

* * * * *

They finished at the Rivers' and drove their separate cars to McDonald's for a late lunch. Bill felt nervous, but there was no place he would rather be at that moment than with Kylee.

"I thought for a moment you were going to faint," she said. Her words were light, but there was an underlying seriousness.

He put a french fry into his mouth, a wry smile on his lips. "I almost did. You know those comics where the person gets hit in the head and sees stars? Well, that was me, standing there with all the stars swirling around."

"Really?"

"Yeah." He laughed and Kylee laughed with him.

After a while Kylee's face became serious. "So what happened back there?"

"A long time ago I wanted to help children like Anna and Jeffery, but then Nicole . . ." He shook his head, not wanting to explain the feelings that were still so raw. "Never mind, I'd rather not talk about that right now. What's important is that I can do some of the surgeries, as many as you want. I won't charge a thing, except where other specialists are involved. But maybe I can get them to donate time as well, and maybe some of the supply companies would be willing to pitch in."

"Thank you."

"You don't have to thank me." Bill knew he was only doing what he should have volunteered to do in the first place.

"So when do we do the surgery?" she asked between sips of her drink. "How much money will we need to start?"

"I can cover the expenses this time."

She frowned. "If you are in this for the long haul—as I hope you are—then we need to pay as we go. If you foot the bill for the other doctors and hospital fees involved, you'll soon go bankrupt—especially if you cut down on your regular practice."

"Agreed, but I can cover Jeffery's case. He'll need a hearing and breathing specialist, but several of the doctors in the Plaza owe me favors; I did free cosmetic surgery years back for a few of their wives. There's a burn department too, and one of the new guys is fairly good, if young. I'm sure I could convince him to assist. He's the sort who would like to be involved. You know, an idealist like you." He raised his hands hastily. "No offense. And when we're through Jeff may not look completely normal, but he'll look and feel a lot better than he does now."

Bill had not helped many burn patients lately, though years ago he had once thought about specializing in that area. All that had ended when Nicole had died, but over the years, he had continued to read and study everything about the subject, as if doing so would somehow alleviate his guilt for not saving her.

Kylee put her hand on his. "I don't think you can understand how much this means to me."

"Oh, yes, I think I might." He watched her take a bite of hamburger.

"What?" she asked, meeting his stare.

I think I love you, he thought. Aloud he said, "I meant what I said about being sorry for leaving you the other night."

She swallowed the food in her mouth. "I'm sorry too. I shouldn't have said what I did."

"Even when you were right?" He knew his voice was slightly bitter. "What must you have thought of me?"

"I don't pretend to understand what you're going through, but I want to. Can you tell me? I mean, we're friends, right?"

Bill suddenly wished they were alone instead of in a crowded restaurant. He longed to take her into his arms, as he had wanted to do from the moment he had arrived at Jeffery's. He wanted to tell her that he had discovered during the past week how much he loved her, that his life meant nothing without her by his side. But did he have the right to say these things when he still yearned for Nicole? Did he have the right when he couldn't even tell her how seeing Jeffery had affected him? Why couldn't he make sense of it all?

There was another fear, so close to the surface that it nearly blotted out all rational thought. The fear that he would win Kylee only to lose her. He couldn't go through that again, he simply couldn't.

Kylee began gathering the remains of the lunch. "Come on, let's go."

Bill needed no second invitation. "Can you take a drive with me?" he asked.

"Yes," she agreed readily, giving Bill hope.

They left her car at the restaurant, and he drove once more to the observatory at Griffith Park. The sun was still high and the city of L.A. had not yet dressed up in her evening lights.

"Here again?" Kylee asked. "We came here on the night of your award banquet."

"Yes." *The night you told me about Emily.* "It loses a lot of its appeal during the day, but it's habit for me to come here."

Kylee settled back in her seat. "But don't you need to go to work or something?"

"I got someone to cover for me. I'll have to work overtime to catch up, but it's worth it."

In the confinement of his Blazer, Bill could smell her perfume. As one, they turned and faced each other. "Tell me," she urged softly. "Is this about Jeffery and why you changed your mind?"

Bill swallowed his fear and spoke from his heart. "No, it's about us. You see, I . . . I care about you. I don't want to lose you. If I'm going to, then I don't want . . . I mean . . ."

"I'm not going anywhere." Her voice was gentle.

He closed his eyes. "Neither was Nicole."

Kylee took his hands and held them until he looked at her. He saw she was crying. "Don't," he said.

"I'm not Nicole, and I know that I could never replace her in your life. But what we have is real. I'm crazy about you."

"I don't want you to be Nicole. She's gone forever."

"I don't believe that. God has a plan. I think we'll see her again in heaven, don't you?"

"No, I don't." He couldn't understand why she insisted on

bringing God into their relationship. "Nicole is gone, so what she wants doesn't matter. That's what I believe. And yet for some stupid reason I feel unfaithful, and now I'm afraid both of losing you and keeping you."

Kylee groaned. "You're not making sense."

Her closeness tempted Bill to forget about conversation, but he knew he had to tell her how he felt, or at least some of it. "I know I'm not making sense. What I'm trying to say is if we continue with this relationship and all goes well, then we'll be together for longer than I even knew Nicole. You'll mean more to me than she did." He trembled as she touched his face, her fingers coming away wet. Funny, he hadn't noticed his own tears. "I know it seems silly," he continued, "but I feel as though I'm betraying her."

"She loved us both. She would want us to be happy. Wherever that may lead us."

He hugged her. "I want to believe that. I really do."

She kissed him then, and all the barriers crashed down like a flood of water. "Oh, Kylee," he breathed, "I think I'm falling in love with you."

"I sort of feel the same way." Her words were a whisper.

Bill kissed her with increasing emotion and her warm lips answered back. His body felt hot inside his jacket, despite the cool breeze coming through his partially opened window. They sat holding each other and overlooking L.A. for a long time, lost in the newness of their love.

Then Kylee shivered. "Could you roll up your window? It's getting chilly."

He laughed, rubbing her arms. "And I thought you were from Minnesota. Don't they have lots of snow?"

"I may have grown up there, but now I always go somewhere warm during the winter. Why do you think I'm in California?"

Her words brought a lot of other questions to his mind. Like where she planned on going next, and where that would leave their relationship. He couldn't make her stay. Fear rose within him. *She said she loves me,* he thought. *I can't have faith in her God, but I can have just a little in her. Besides, she needs me for the children.*

Bill knew this last thought did her an injustice, but it made him feel remarkably better. He kissed her again deeply. She clung to him, and a tenderness he had thought long dead encompassed his entire body. What was that feeling? Love? No, something greater. *Maybe I'm insane.* He shrugged the experience aside as she drew away.

"So what now?" she asked.

Bill knew she was asking about their future but he chose to misunderstand, to give himself more time. "I guess I should check in at work. I'd like to see when we can get Jeffery in. If we work fast, maybe we can do it so we can have the bandages off for Christmas. Those from his first surgery, that is. I'll know more when I've examined him."

Gratitude glowed in her eyes, and Bill was glad that he had finally found the strength to do what she needed, what they both needed. Nicole would be proud.

He took Kylee back to McDonald's and reluctantly watched her drive away. The fear of losing her returned, but it was smaller now, overshadowed by her love.

CHAPTER 14

Kylee's mind reeled with the events of the day. So much had gone wrong, but then so much else had gone right. She felt blessed and protected. *And Bill loves me!* She had a feeling that the going wouldn't be easy, but she wouldn't give up on him. Once he had believed in God. Once he had been free of bitterness and pain. He could be so again. *If only he would pray,* she thought. *Then he would feel the Lord's presence and His love.*

She went into her own room and knelt by her bed, resting her arms on the blankets. Her thankfulness poured out to the Lord. Sometimes enduring to the end was all she could do, but by answering her need to help the children, the Lord had shown her once again how much He cared about her individual situation. With His support, she would continue.

When she arose from her knees, she felt refreshed and content. There were still problems, but now with Bill volunteering to enter the battle, her burden was lighter. She looked happily around the apartment. A stack of paperwork awaited her attention on the desk in her room, but she had other plans.

"I know just what this place is missing."

In her hall closet she found the three large boxes, worn now with years of being hauled around to different cities or storage sheds when she went overseas. On the boxes she had scrawled *CHRISTMAS* in red marker.

Next, she pulled out her tree from under the bed and also a box of ornaments. After the pieces were put together, the tree was shorter and thinner than she thought a tree should be, but the ornaments made it look nice. She had to tape three more of the sagging tree branches so they would poke out right, but that was nothing new. She had bought the now-dilapidated thing in college and couldn't bear to throw it away. Every year she taped a few more branches into place. This year she had planned to buy a new one, but now she needed to save all the money she could until she helped the children enough to pay herself a small salary.

She went to work on the other boxes, and in short order her small apartment was glistening with tinsel, bells, angels, and more. She lined the mantle, the back of the sofa, the coffee table, the top of the kitchen cupboards, the windows, and the door with colored lights. Over the years she had collected far too many decorations for the small apartment, but she put them all out anyway. Finished, she stood back to admire her handiwork, and had to admit that the effect was rather garish. But the whole scene raised her spirits further.

Now what she needed was a candle or incense to make the room smell like the tree was real. Even she could afford that. She swept up her purse, but as she opened her apartment door she found Bill standing outside, his hand raised to ring the bell. "Yie!" Kylee gasped. "You scared me!"

"Oh, are you just leaving? And I was beginning to think you were psychic. May I come in?"

Kylee hesitated. What would he think? "I'm not sure you're ready for this."

"Ready for what?" He pushed his way inside and gave a long, low whistle. "What happened here? Did a Christmas bomb go off?" From the end table he picked up a candle in the shape of a fat snowman and tossed it from one hand to the other.

"No. And be careful with that," she said, rescuing the snowman. She set it carefully on a pile of cotton next to a matching Santa. "But wait, you haven't seen the full effect." She turned on the lights.

Bill whistled again. "You never told me you were decoratively handicapped."

"I prefer to think of it as differently decorative." She sniffed, before winking and giving him a wry smile. "I know it's a lot all at once, but I love my decorations and I love Christmas. This place is just a little small."

"Hmmm," he said, obviously succumbing to tact.

"Hey, why are you here anyway? You were going to work."

"I did. My substitute had it covered, and I missed you so I left again."

Kylee could see he was telling the truth and felt suddenly shy. "Well, you should have come earlier and you could have helped me with the tree."

"It does look a bit lopsided."

"I like it that way."

He peered closer. "And I never knew that trees used masking tape. It must be a new brand."

Kylee's laughter bubbled up and over. "Oh, shut up, will you? I'd like to see *your* decorations."

"I don't have any."

She blinked. "You don't?"

"No, nothing."

A sad tenderness filled Kylee's heart. She couldn't imagine not having any Christmas decorations. Even someone who claimed not to believe in God could have lights and a Santa. "Well, we can solve that." She began putting some of her things back into one of the discarded boxes. "You can afford lights, can't you?"

"Wait, wait, wait! I don't know if I could live like this till January."

"Trust me," she said.

He looked at her oddly. "I do."

"Then come on."

They went first to the store to buy more strings of colored lights, as well as a few green garlands with white lights woven along the lengths. Then Kylee insisted he buy a real tree. "What do I need a tree for?" he asked.

"For my ornaments, of course."

Bill raised his hands in defeat. "All right. Whatever your heart desires."

"Whatever?" Kylee felt her heart thumping strangely. "You better be careful what you say. I might believe you." She purposely made the words light, but meant them all the same. He had said that he loved her, and while she knew that was a tremendous step for him, she craved more. Marriage, another child, even the white picket fence—or something similar. But there was still much left unsaid, feelings that he hadn't shared. And no matter what, she wouldn't settle for a relationship that didn't include marriage. That made it too easy to walk away.

Of course, marriage hadn't prevented Raymond from leaving her.

Bill isn't Raymond. Bill left once when I needed him, but he came back. A sobering thought followed: *But is he back forever? And how can it be forever if he doesn't even believe in God?*

She still worried about his lack of religious beliefs, but he could change. Or was she fooling herself? Was she so tired of being alone that she couldn't put the Lord first anymore? Kylee sighed, not wanting to hear the answer.

Bill broke into her thoughts. "Is something wrong? You suddenly went quiet."

"No, nothing's wrong. I think I'm more than a little tired. It's been a long day."

"Well, why don't you come back to my place and I'll fix you a nice dinner? I can cook a thing or two."

"Good idea. That way I can decorate."

He groaned but there was a twinkle in his dark eyes. "I guess, if you must." He made a last check of the tree, assuring himself it was securely tied to the roof of the Blazer. "It's a good thing I didn't drive the BMW today."

Kylee laughed. "I'll say. We might have scratched the paint."

"Can't have that." He started the engine and eased the Blazer onto the road. "Although, I may have to sell the BMW if you keep coming up with children to help."

"You can share my Camry," she offered.

"That old thing?"

"It gets me where I want to go."

"So far."

Kylee grinned. "Isn't that what counts?"

"You win," he said. "So what are we going to eat for dinner?"

"More s'mores?"

He snorted. "No, and stop sounding so hopeful."

"Dang. Well, maybe for dessert." They drove in silence for a while and then Bill reached over for her hand, holding it tight. "I'm glad you're here."

She smiled. "So am I."

They spent a wonderful evening cooking dinner together, eating s'mores, and decorating the house. Though she craved to discover his innermost thoughts, Kylee tried to make their first evening in love fun instead of overly serious. Bill seemed to relax, and to her surprise began to talk about his childhood.

"You and your brother were really close, weren't you?" she asked.

"Yes. But he's got his family now." He winked at her. "And I have you."

Kylee felt warmth fill her entire being. Everything was almost perfect. "How did your parents celebrate Christmas?"

"Oh, the usual. Trees, candy, the whole bit. But Christmas then wasn't anywhere near as commercialized as it is today."

She couldn't help probing. "What about church?"

"We went to mass." That was all he would say, and Kylee hesitated to push further.

She didn't let Bill kiss her again until he took her back to her apartment. She knew he had wanted to, but she kept avoiding him, afraid of the intensity of her own emotions. There would be plenty of time to talk about the physical part of their relationship in the future. For now, she wanted to take everything slowly, to savor each moment of her newfound love.

* * * * *

Bill woke up early Thursday morning, despite his late night with Kylee. He stretched in his bed. Bed? It must have been only the second or third night he had slept in his bed since he had met Kylee. No more traumatic nights sleeping on the couch and watching TV until his brain froze. He wished Kylee could be lying next to him, but he knew her well enough to know that meant further commitment. Yet today the idea didn't send him into fits of guilt as it had before.

How odd. When Kylee had insisted that Nicole still lived on in heaven, he worried it might make his guilt intensify. Yet it hadn't. "You would understand, wouldn't you, Nicole?" he said aloud, and felt the strange emotion of the day before fill his heart, chest, and then his entire body with warmth.

Whistling, he pulled himself from bed and went down the stairs, which now had green garlands and white lights circling the handrails. Kylee had wired huge gold bows to the garlands at regular intervals, and the effect was elegant—far different from the mishmash of her apartment. Despite himself, Bill stopped and plugged in the lights. It looked good. Maybe he would even buy more decorations.

In the kitchen, he began unloading the dishwasher as he always did every other morning. This time it was full of the dishes he and Kylee had used, instead of the few items he normally used. What a magical evening! He would have to call her as soon as he had a chance.

* * * * *

Kylee awoke for the first time in a long time with nothing to do. Oh, there was the ever-constant paperwork for Children's Hope, but nothing urgent enough to get her out of bed. She lay in her bed instead, thinking dreamily of Bill. *I love him. I really do.*

Have I ever been so happy?

Yes, when she had given birth to Emily. Then her angel had died, and Kylee had never dared imagine a day when she would feel as happy as she did today.

The phone rang, and hoping it was Bill, she rolled across the bed and reached for the phone. "Hello, Bill?"

"No, it's me, Suzy. I take it that means Bill and you are still seeing each other?"

"We are." Kylee settled onto her pillows. "He's really come around. He's agreed to help the children and everything."

"That's what I'm calling about. I realize it happened a while ago, but only last night did I hear about what happened. Becky told me. I'm so sorry about them taking off with the money like that. I want to kill them! Have they found them yet?"

"No. And I don't think they will. Elaina's too smart. But it's going to be okay. I'll have to work really hard, but—"

"I'm sending you a check."

"You don't have to."

"I know that. But I also know that you're likely living on next to nothing. My check is to help you pay the rent until you get back on your feet. But don't worry about repaying me. I don't need it."

"Thank you so much, Suzy," Kylee answered, her throat choked with emotion. "You really are a friend. I wish I could hug you!"

"Well, you can. Mauro and I are flying into town a week from Saturday and we'll be staying until Monday. I'm getting worried about my church attendance. I've had to work far too many Sundays. But that's all ending now. I'm requesting my fair share of weekends off. No more taking others' shifts. Mauro's going to do the same thing. Hey, that reminds me of another reason I called. Do you think I could bunk up at your place for that weekend? I'm letting Mauro stay at my apartment since the other girls will be out on flights. But I can't stay there because, well, you know."

Kylee laughed. "Of course I know. Old Mrs. Peabody next door'd call it a den of iniquity and get you kicked out."

"Exactly."

"How does Mauro feel about that?"

"He agrees, of course. He's really a good guy. His parents raised him right, even if it was in a different church."

Kylee thought of Bill. "Does he believe in God?"

"Of course he does. I couldn't imagine loving someone who didn't believe in God. There would be too many problems, too many conflicts. So are you going to let me stay, or not?"

"Of course you can stay. I'd love to have you."

"Okay then, I'll see you Saturday."

"Plan for lunch on Sunday, or something," Kylee said.

"For your cooking? It's a deal. Will Bill be there?"

"Yes, I'm sure he will. I'll invite him."

"Good. I'll be glad to meet him. And I have a surprise for you. Good news"

"Tell me!"

"Nope. Have to wait. Dang, I've got to go. They're paging me. See ya."

Kylee hung up the phone and lay back on the bed, staring at the ceiling. What news could Suzy have? With her it could be anything from a letter to Santa to an earth-shattering announcement. She loved to spring surprises on people. Kylee couldn't count the times Suzy had appeared on her doorstep with no warning.

So what was different about this time? For one, she needed a place to stay. No, that couldn't be it. Was Mauro getting baptized? Now that could be it. Kylee frowned, remembering Suzy's words, "I couldn't imagine loving someone who didn't believe in God. There would be too many problems."

Bill didn't believe in God, or if by some chance there was a God, he didn't believe that such an exalted being would care about mere mortals. But that could change, couldn't it? Or was she only fooling herself? Would she be willing to live a life of attending church alone? What would happen to their children?

"Stop it," Kylee said aloud. "It's not as if he's asked you to marry him." Would he even want to get married? His marriage with Nicole had lasted only two days and he had been alone since then. Maybe over the last five years he had grown too set in his bachelorhood. Kylee tried again to push her doubts aside, but it was difficult. She was relieved when the phone rang again.

"What are you doing?" Bill asked.

Kylee looked down at her nightgown and stifled a laugh. "Oh, nothing much. Just about to go through some papers."

"Well, I called to tell you I've scheduled Jeffery for a week from Monday on the twentieth. Hope that's all right."

"It's wonderful. I'll call and tell Mr. Rivers right now. Oh, that reminds me, I need to call and see how Anna and Mrs. Johnson are doing."

"She'll be pretty swollen for the next week," he said. "But Dr. Nelson has a good reputation, and she should look a lot better than she did."

"This is so exciting!"

"You better not read the local paper then."

Kylee's smile vanished. "Oh, no. What now?"

"A very negative article about the charity."

"But they printed my release. I don't understand what they're doing. This shouldn't even be news anymore. Read it to me, okay?"

"You sure?"

"I can take it."

"Uh, let's see . . . 'Children's charity swindles millions.' That's the title. Underneath it says, 'Children's Hope Fund of Los Angeles, California has stolen millions of dollars from unsuspecting donors. Several months ago the charity launched an aggressive campaign that brought their company to the attention of the entire nation. People across the country donated in amounts from five dollars to one million dollars. The money was supposed to go to children who desperately need surgeries, but instead the charity administrators, Troy Stutts and Elaina Rinehart, used funds for their own gain. There's no telling how much they have taken over the years, but an estimated 24.5 million dollars was recently transferred to overseas banks. Stutts and Rinehart have left the country, but it is uncertain whether or not they are still operating this scam through employees. While the fund-raising organizer for Children's Hope, Kylee Stuart, is still actively seeking donations, authorities from the FBI are urging people to stop handing over their hard-earned cash. To date no children have been helped by the charity.'" Bill paused and then added, "There's a bit more of the same. Plus a few nasty comments from some angry people who donated."

"A little truth mixed with some big lies. Elaina and Troy *did* help many children, and they never stole before—I can vouch for that. And to insinuate that I'm still collecting money to send to them is too unbelievable for words."

"Do you want me to call them?" Bill asked quietly.

"No. I'll go down there myself. Maybe I can get them to listen to my point of view. I'll even show them the e-mails I've exchanged with the FBI. That ought to add authenticity."

"I'm really sorry, Kylee."

"Me too. But thanks for being there for me. I know it's not easy for you to help Jeffery."

He laughed. "A lot easier than I thought." There was a loaded silence and then, "I missed you when I woke up," Bill said, his voice tender. "I imagined what it would be like to have you next to me."

"You did? And then what?"

"And then I went downstairs and unloaded the dishwasher. We certainly used a lot of dishes last night. Usually I run it nearly empty." His voice had returned to its normal timbre. "Hey, what about dinner tonight?"

"Your place or mine?"

"How about Chinese? I know this little restaurant near your place, and the food's good."

"What about money? You're already going to take a big hit with Jeffery's surgery."

"Anyone can afford this place. Besides, I'm not going broke for a long time yet. I'm a plastic surgeon, and you should see my surgery schedule the rest of this week." He chuckled. "Pre-Christmas presents, you know. Not only do people have time off, many of them have to use the rest of the funds in their Cafeteria plans before January, or they lose them. This is my busiest time of the year. So how about it?"

"I'd love to. Thanks."

"I'll come by after work. Not sure when I'll get done, though."

"I'll be here. I have work to do here, so whenever you're ready, come over."

"Okay, I will." He hesitated again. "If you need me, call. You have the number."

"I will." Kylee hung up the phone, warmth flooding her senses. It was kind of silly that he worried about her. She could certainly take care of herself. Yet after so long on her own, it felt wonderful to have a man other than her church leaders be concerned for her welfare. Her religion was important to her, but maybe she could give Bill a few weeks and see what happened. He was a good man.

She sat up and swung her feet off the bed. Time to face the world.

After calling Mr. Rivers and Mrs. Johnson, Kylee went down to the newspaper office. She was interviewed almost immediately by a reporter, a sure sign of a hot story. When she left the office, she felt confident they would print an accurate version.

She drove somewhat reluctantly to the post office where she checked her box, fearing to find stacks of letters from the people on her charity lists, censuring her for losing their contributions. Instead, there were only a few letters with donations that had trickled in from the TV commercial before it had been pulled. She sighed with relief, although she knew that the dreaded letters probably hadn't had time to arrive yet. Kylee drove to the bank and deposited the new donations. The total of the checks was less than a hundred dollars, but anything would help the children.

Back at the apartment she busied herself with paperwork, but there wasn't much left from her frantic letter-writing sessions the two previous weekends. Suddenly in her hand was the list of children waiting for Children's Hope to answer their dreams. She couldn't stop herself from looking at the next name—Chantel, the baby with Apert syndrome. Kylee remembered well the infant from the video shoot. Elaina had said that she had bumped the child to the top of the list because of the immediacy of her need for surgery. Chantel would need several operations on her skull throughout her life to avoid mental retardation. She also needed surgery on her mittened hands and feet to make fingers and toes. It would be a long process, but the memory of the angelic baby on the video tugged at Kylee's heart. Chantel reminded her of Emily, of her deep longing for another baby of her own. "It won't be long now," Kylee said aloud to Chantel. "We'll get you fixed up."

When Bill came to pick her up, she told him about Chantel. "I remember that baby," he said. "From your video."

"You've got a good memory."

"Not really, she just stood out. You'll need a craniofacial surgeon and about seven other specialists to help her. I'll be glad to help with the parts I'm qualified for."

Kylee hugged him. "Thank you so much. I don't know how or why you changed your mind about all this, but I'm grateful."

"It seems the right thing to do."

Kylee's heart filled with hope. "The right thing? That sort of makes it seem like you believe in God. I mean, the right thing versus the wrong thing."

Bill shook his head, his lips curved in a gentle smile. Instead of replying, he asked, "How'd it go at the newspaper?"

"Good, I think. But I'm sorry, your name might be in the paper tomorrow."

He laughed. "Well, I guess I'd better get used to that if I'm going to help you. At least now they should have the real story."

"Yeah, and I'll bet they'll call it late-breaking news even though they printed my news release two Sundays ago—way in the back of the paper."

"Probably."

The Chinese restaurant was perfect, and the mood between them romantic. But Kylee couldn't help thinking about Suzy's comments and what Bill's attitude against religion might mean to their relationship in the long run. He didn't seem particularly antagonistic toward her church, rather apathetic about all churches in general. For Kylee's part, her faith in Jesus Christ had been a mainstay in her life since Emily's death. Could she really consider having a serious—hopefully a lifetime—relationship with someone who couldn't share that part of her life? Though she had once thought Bill's love might be enough, now she wasn't sure. She had made a terrible decision by marrying Raymond. What if she was making a similar mistake with Bill?

He hasn't asked you to marry him, she reminded herself.

"Do you like children?" she asked.

Bill chuckled. "Where'd that come from? We were talking about seasonings."

"Well, I guess I wondered if you and Nicole had planned on having children."

"Yes, we did. A few. You know she was nuts about kids."

"I knew that, but I didn't know how you felt."

"I like children. At least the few children I know."

"I mean, you didn't want to do any surgeries before and—"

"It wasn't the children," Bill retorted.

"Then what?"

There was a flash of irritation in his face that made Kylee feel rebuked, as though he had told her she had no business delving into his feelings. But if she didn't, who would? He said he loved her, and that meant sharing their inner emotions, didn't it?

Her hurt must have shown in her face because Bill sighed and reached out to touch her hand. "I'm sorry. I guess you deserve to know, but I'm not very proud of my reasons." He shook his head. "I didn't want them to depend on me. It doesn't make sense but I didn't want to have to care about them. To . . . to . . ."

"Feel?" Kylee supplied.

"Yeah, I suppose that's it."

"Because of Nicole."

"Yes." He paused. "Those children need someone warm and loving to help them. Someone who will care about seeing them through. I couldn't do that. And I didn't want to even try. All I saw when I looked at them was Nicole's flesh on that day in France, as dark and full of ashes as my dreams."

"So what happened to change your mind?" Kylee felt she was

beginning to understand him.

He didn't say anything for a long time, but stirred the Chinese food with his chopsticks. "You happened."

"So you want to help the children because of me."

"Hey, it was a start." He gave her a small grin before becoming serious again. "But that's not all. Someone—my brother actually—reminded me of how I had once wanted to help children when I was in school. I had forgotten that." He dropped his chopsticks and put his hand over hers. "Truth is, I didn't make the decision until I saw Jeffery yesterday. I had come to convince you to forgive me, to accept me as I was, despite the fact that I didn't want to help the children. I thought maybe I could agree to do something minor, if that's what it took to get you to talk to me." Bill grimaced. "I know that doesn't sound very good of me, but it was all I could do then."

"But you told Jeffery you wanted to help him."

He nodded. "That wasn't planned. When I saw him standing there with that ragged mitt, I wanted to run away. But he looked so scared and helpless . . . I knew I could help him. I could make a difference. He wasn't Nicole, and ignoring his need couldn't bring her back."

"But maybe helping him can—at least in some way."

His eyes met hers for a long, silent moment. "Yes. You do understand."

"I think I do." Kylee remembered the moment she had let the love of the Savior heal the wounds of Emily's death and Raymond's betrayal. Yes, she knew intimately the feeling of tossing away fear for the hope of a new future. Bill's decision to help the children meant that he was finally ready to move out of the past. And perhaps into her future.

His grip on her hand tightened. "You've been through so much, and I figure if you could go through what you did with Emily and still have the ability to love, then I can also find that strength. Even if I have to lean on you for a while. I can help those children. And I love you, Kylee. I really do."

"I love you too," she whispered. There was no going back now. She loved him completely, and either they would continue together and be happy, or they would both get hurt. Would it be her religion that separated them? *Oh, why did I have to talk to Suzy today?*

After dinner Bill took her home and said good night. "I have to get up early to make up for the time I was off yesterday." He kissed her, and her doubts were banished to the deep recesses of her mind.

"I'll see you tomorrow?" he asked against her ear, their bodies pressed together.

Kylee laughed. "My place or yours?"

"Yours."

When he left, Kylee stood for a long while staring out the window into the dark, starless night. Her heart felt full and tender, but for some reason she didn't know if she should laugh or cry.

CHAPTER 15

The next day the newspaper printed an article about Children's Hope on the front page. Kylee read through it quickly, praying for the best. While still referring to the missing millions, the reporter corrected the previous misinformation and focused more on the children, and how money was still needed so they could be helped. At one point in the article, Bill and several other specialists were mentioned by name:

William Dubrey of Newport Beach, Curtis Nelson of Los Angeles, and Gerald Torgeson of Glendale are just a few of the plastic surgeons, dentists, and other specialists who are teaming up with Children's Hope. These doctors are donating their time without compensation. All are dedicated to seeing that any incoming funds buy as many supplies as possible to help additional children.

While the entire article had a positive vein, Kylee loved the ending the best, although she supposed that some could consider it stretching the truth: "Despite the controversy that has surrounded this charity, it is now under new administration and has been approved by the FBI. All donations are encouraged."

She called Bill immediately to read him the article, but he had just finished reading it himself. "So you're approved by the FBI, huh?" he said with a laugh. "I didn't know they approved charities."

"Well, obviously, they did mine. Don't you believe everything you read?"

"It's a great article," Bill told her. "And I'm happy for you. When I come over tonight I'll bring a bottle of . . . hmm . . . grape juice to celebrate."

"Okay, and I'll cook something wonderful. I hope you like fish." She had to fight to keep the laughter from her voice.

Bill wasn't fooled. "I'll eat it if you eat it first."

"Okay, no fish. How about lasagne?"

"Now you're talking."

* * * * *

Every night for the rest of that week, and most of the next, Kylee had dinner with Bill. And each time she saw him, she loved him more. They laughed together, sang silly songs, and talked until her throat was sore. Kylee hadn't been so happy since she had first found out she was pregnant with Emily. Occasionally, she caught herself dreaming about having another baby, hers and Bill's.

On the morning of the eighteenth of December, the Saturday Suzy would be flying into town, Kylee made another stop at the post office, dreading what she would find. Sure enough, there was a mess of letters scattered in the large P.O. box. She gathered them up in a thick orderly stack, her heart thumping as she recognized many of the addresses from her special lists of people. No doubt they were writing to censure her, to demand reimbursement—or worse. She had been assured by the FBI that there could be no legal action taken against her, but she worried what she might have to endure if someone decided to sue her.

In the car, she read the first letter. Tears rolled down her cheeks, her emotions too full for anything else. Inside, with a kind letter of consolation, was a very generous check made out to Children's Hope.

Eagerly now, Kylee opened the other envelopes and found more of the same. Many of the caring people on her lists had not blamed or condemned her for the events, but had opened their hearts and wallets to help her continue her mission without Elaina and Troy.

There were a few spiteful letters, and even one that threatened her with legal action, but Kylee was so filled with the magnanimity of the others that she barely noticed. She immediately drove to Bill's, anxious to tell him about the donations in person.

"Thank heaven you're home," she said when he opened the door.

"Kylee! Are you okay?"

For an answer, she piled the letters in his hands. "Look."

Bill read them and cried with her. "This is wonderful! I'm so happy for you."

"For us. Now we can help more children."

He hugged her. "Thank you, Kylee."

"For what?"

"For coming here and sharing it with me."

"You were the first person that came to mind. Although I did think of Suzy afterward. She's flying in this evening."

"Oh, that reminds me. About lunch with your friend tomorrow—would you rather have it here instead of at your apartment? We could use the dining room like we did at Thanksgiving."

"I'd love that!" She kissed him thoroughly on the mouth.

"Mmm. Maybe I'll let you use my dining room every day."

She laughed. "That reminds me. I'd better get food for tomorrow. I'm about out of everything edible."

"I'd go with you, but I have a surgery scheduled."

"On Saturday?"

He shrugged. "It was the one I was supposed to do on Monday when I'm going to do Jeffery."

She kissed him again. "You're the best, you know?"

"Well, no, but you can keep telling me. I could probably handle that."

She laughed and punched his shoulder.

"Hey, I have time for a quick breakfast," he said. "Have you eaten?"

Kylee had eaten but she wanted to stay with Bill. "I could force down an egg or two," she said with a smile. "But then I'm going to call Julie and tell her she just might be able to have her old job back at Children's Hope."

"Now isn't that jumping the gun a little?" Bill asked.

"I'm not hiring her again yet. I just think she'll be pleased to know."

* * * * *

Suzy didn't show up at Kylee's apartment until late that evening, just after Kylee had bid goodnight to Bill. They had shared a pizza at her apartment after his last surgery, and he had wanted to see a movie, but she insisted they wait at her apartment for Suzy.

"Besides," she added. "I have to get up early for church tomorrow. And those boys are a handful. Are you sure you don't want to come? You could keep them in line."

He grinned. "Maybe sometime. Tomorrow I'm going to sleep in. It's been a long week. And I bet you do just fine with those boys."

Kylee had stifled her sigh and kissed him goodbye. Doubts again assailed her about their ultimate compatibility. "He deserves a rest," she told herself, her voice loud in the small kitchen. Frowning, she went to her room to set up the small portable cot which she kept under her bed. She also changed the sheets on her bed, planning to offer it to Suzy.

Suzy was alone when she arrived. "It's so good to see you!" she exclaimed, enveloping Kylee in an enthusiastic hug. "Sorry I'm so late, but I had a host of errands piled up at the apartment. We even had an eviction notice on the door! It took me all night to track down our landlord and convince him it was a mistake. We had the money in the apartment, but everyone had forgotten to give it to him."

"Good thing you came home."

"I'll say."

"So where's Mauro?"

"I left him at the apartment. He was really tired and I didn't want him to have to drive back there alone. You know, in a strange town. I'll stop and get him for church though, so you'll meet him then." She settled on the couch. "Now I know we've got to get to bed, but tell me, what's going on?"

They ended up talking far into the night, laughing and crying as they shared what had happened in their lives since their last good talk. But Kylee felt Suzy was holding something back. "What's up, Suzy? You seem different."

Suzy smiled and her eyes misted over. "I was going to wait and tell you with Mauro, but were getting married!" She dug a ring box out of her purse. "See?"

"So that's the news you mentioned on the phone."

"Yep, that's it."

"That's wonderful! At least I think it is. I mean, I haven't met him yet. But if he passed your father's approval . . ."

"He did. Especially since he's joining the Church." Suzy gazed dreamily at the ceiling. "Oh, he's perfect, and I love him so much!"

Kylee hugged her friend, wishing she could say the same about Bill. In many ways he was her dream man. If only he could accept God.

* * * * *

The next morning they drove separately to church. Suzy showed up a short time after Kylee, accompanied by a blond-haired man with blue eyes. The pilot was deeply tanned, extremely handsome, and obviously in love with Suzy. With Suzy's long blonde locks and matching blue eyes, they made a striking couple.

"It's nice to meet you," Mauro said. He turned to Suzy. "You didn't tell me she was so pretty. And she has green eyes."

Suzy laughed. "He's got a thing with green eyes," she told Kylee.

"I do not."

Suzy stuck her tongue at him. "Do too."

Mauro kissed her.

"Okay, you win."

Kylee smiled. "You two are nuts—perfect for each other."

"Not quite," Mauro said. "I'm not baptized. But I will be soon."

"Congratulations." Kylee slapped him on the back. "It looks like we have two things to celebrate at lunch."

Although she was happy for her friend, a lump formed in Kylee's throat during the meeting. How she would love Bill to sit through the services beside her. And not just for her sake, but because he believed in God. Pushing the thoughts aside, Kylee threw herself into the services and then into her Sunday School lesson for the youth.

After church was over, Kylee stopped at her apartment for the crock pot roast and potatoes she had begun cooking early that morning. Suzy and Mauro followed her to Bill's condo in the old car Suzy kept around to use on her few days off from the airlines. "This must be serious," Mauro called to Kylee as she got out of her car to punch the gate code for them. "I mean, it must be if you have his gate code."

Kylee laughed. "Well, it's a long story. And you're not hearing it from me."

"Nor me," Suzy said.

"Then I'll have to ask Bill."

And he did as soon as the introductions were made. Bill laughed. "Oh, that was because Kylee once climbed over the gate wearing a long dress, you know, one of those tight, sequined things."

"She didn't!"

"Oh, yes she did," Bill answered. "And I'm still waiting to get my copy of the event from the security guys."

"You are?" Kylee gasped.

"Naw, but I just had to see your face when I said it."

The group talked and laughed, enjoying each other's company while Kylee mixed bacon bits and her special olive oil dressing into the salad. But during the meal itself the topic switched to religious beliefs, and an almost palpable tension filled the air.

"Kylee, do you know how long I've waited to find someone who shares my beliefs?" Suzy said. "I almost can't believe I finally did! I wanted to be able to worship together, to teach our children about God. As a flight attendant I've met a lot of confused people, and I didn't want my children to grow up like that. I was so relieved that Mauro believes in God. Though I have to confess that I was already half in love with him before I knew."

"I'm not too sure I believe in God." Bill took a second helping of Kylee's roast.

There was a lengthy silence and then Mauro asked. "Why?"

"Well, what proof do you have that He exists?"

Mauro straightened up in his chair and took the challenge. "What proof do you have that He doesn't?"

"Crime, hate, abuse, children going hungry," Bill replied dryly. "The list goes on."

"What about the beauty in the world? How about love, sacrifice, and the good things that go on? How about the intricate workings of the universe? Could that perfect system be an accident?" Mauro's voice showed amazement. "You as a doctor would know how unlikely that would be."

"It could happen," Bill said, "in such a big universe."

"Still not likely," Mauro insisted. "The odds are too incredible."

Bill shrugged. "I have a brother who is also a member of your religion, and we've talked about this many times. I believe there are many solar systems in our galaxy that have planets with conditions to sustain life. And many more in other galaxies across the universe. Life on this planet isn't so difficult to believe."

"But it is if you know what's involved. It's almost impossible." Mauro stared intently at Bill, as if willing him to understand and believe. "We require exact conditions—air, water, heat, light. Not to mention how we got here in the first place. The whole evolution idea simply hasn't been proven. There's still the missing link."

"I didn't say the life on other planets would be human." Bill's mouth twitched with a hint of a smile. "They could breathe methane gases for all I know."

"Bill watches a lot of *Star Trek,*" Kylee interjected, hoping to diffuse the building strain. Tears of frustration were close to the surface.

"I do," Bill admitted. "But just because someone on earth dreamed up the series, that doesn't mean other species don't exist out there. Even your Bible says that God created *man* in His image. By that explanation, He could have created a ton of other sentient life forms that weren't man, couldn't He?"

Mauro chuckled without mirth. "I never thought of it that way. I can only tell you how I feel, that man here and on a lot of other worlds was created by God in His image."

"Well, I don't think anyone created them. Or that if there is a divine being or beings that they would waste time doing it." Bill's words were polite, but firm. Guests or no, he obviously wasn't backing down.

"We're His children; that's why God is concerned with us. It's not a waste of time for Him," Mauro insisted.

Kylee coughed loudly. "That's enough of that topic, I think. We'll just have to agree to disagree. Anyone want dessert?"

"I do," Suzy replied, casting Kylee a grateful glance. "But before I do, I have to tell you, Bill, that your Christmas decorations are simply beautiful. Especially compared to that array at Kylee's. Have you seen her place since she put up the decorations?"

Bill grinned. "Where the Christmas bomb exploded? Yeah, I've seen it."

"And that tree with all the masking tape . . ."

The tension between them dissolved, but Kylee still wanted to cry. She loved Bill, yet they could share none of the things Suzy talked about. No Sunday worship, no discussion of blessings, no joint prayer. And what of their children? As she taught them about God, would he teach them to rely on the arm of flesh? When they faced tragedy, would they continue in faith or run away to another country and change their names?

She hardly noticed as lunch ended and Suzy and Mauro made ready to leave, full of thanks and compliments for the meal. "I'll meet you back at your apartment later tonight," Suzy said.

"Don't wait up for her," Mauro added.

Suzy laughed. "Oh, no you don't. I have to be in before ten. Remember, we both have early flights in the morning."

After they left, Kylee picked up a handful of dishes and walked slowly into the kitchen, still deep in thought. Bill followed with another stack. "Nice people," he commented.

Kylee put a plate in the dishwasher and said nothing.

"They'll be good together, don't you think? Especially since they both work for the airlines."

Kylee rinsed off bits of potatoes sticking to a glass serving bowl.

"We'll have to get together with them again sometime."

She set another plate in the dishwasher, a little too forcefully.

"What's wrong, Kylee?"

"Nothing."

"Tell me."

"I said nothing."

"You *said* nothing was wrong, but your actions are saying something else." He left his dishes on the counter and put his arms around her. "I think we're both adult enough to be honest. What happened? I think the lunch went well."

"It was all the talk about God," she said, seeing that he wasn't going to let her alone.

"I didn't offend them. It was just a discussion."

"I know, but it made me think how you would explain it to any children you might have."

"So?"

"I believe in God," Kylee said. "I don't think I would like my children to not know Him."

"So teach them to believe in God."

"It wouldn't do any good if their father didn't believe. That's too confusing."

"It's giving them a choice."

She broke away from his grasp and stepped away. "I don't see it like that. I mean, how will we teach them to be honest or moral, if we can't teach them to believe in God? If God doesn't exist, then why be moral at all?"

"I don't jump into the sack with every woman I desire." His voice was hard.

Kylee stared at him in frustration. "I know you don't, but you had a good upbringing, didn't you? Your parents were faithfully married and they believed in God. I just think that religion helps children with the choices they'll have to make. Life's hard enough as it is."

"So you're saying you won't marry me because our children won't have a good sex education?"

"Marry you?" Despite the growing numbness in her heart, Kylee seized on the words. "You never said anything about marriage."

"I didn't? Well, we're talking about children, our children, aren't we? I guess I thought my intentions were obvious. Yes, I want to marry you. It's driving me crazy not to be with you." He approached and put his arms tentatively around her, kissing her softly on the cheeks, throat, and mouth. Kylee wanted to succumb to the emotions surging in her heart and body, but there was too much at stake.

"I might be difficult to live with," Bill said in her ear. "I've not had a roommate since I came to America, but I can adjust. I promise to make things work. I love you, Kylee, and I want to marry you. I waited years to marry Nicole, but I waited too long. I don't want to do that now. I want to take advantage of the years we have left. We never know what might happen."

Kylee broke away. "What *might* happen? See, there it is again. I want to be married for forever. I don't want to settle for this life and, poof, nothing more. Heaven does exist, Bill, and I want to be with you there, too."

"Then marry me, and if there's a heaven we'll go there together. What's the problem?"

"If you don't believe in a heaven, how can you go there with me?"

"We'll just go."

"It doesn't work that way. Going to heaven takes more effort than that! How do you expect to live with a Master you don't know and haven't served?"

"Haven't served?" Color tinged his face. "I've always done what I think is right! I'm even to the point where I can help the children you represent, not just because I love you, but because I'm willing to risk their disappointment and their hopes. I've opened my heart. Not served! I have served. Even you have to admit that."

"Yes," she said miserably. "I know you have. You are the most wonderful person I've ever met, and that's why I don't understand why you don't have any faith."

"Faith never got me anywhere," he answered bitterly.

"It might have helped you face Nicole's death."

"I have you for that, don't I?" Now there was a note of desperation in his voice that tore at Kylee's heart.

"I can't be everything to you, Bill. I want to be, but I can't. And I don't know what to do, but I have to make the right decision. I love you, but I can't marry a man who doesn't believe in God. I just can't."

Kylee fled from the kitchen, snatching her purse from the hat rack by the door. Tears fell so quickly that she couldn't see where she was going.

"Don't leave!" Bill called after her. "How do you know that running away is the right choice? Maybe your God wants you to stay." But she continued, afraid that if she looked into his face once more, she wouldn't have the courage to leave.

She hopped into her car and drove until she was sure he hadn't followed. Then she pulled to the side of the road and rested her head on the steering wheel. "I've waited too long to find someone as special as Bill," she said forlornly. "I don't know what to do."

* * * * *

Bill slept on the couch that night. He was angry. No, furious. And mad and hurt. Kylee had betrayed him by allowing him to love her, by allowing him to pledge his life to her, only to run away. *I've lost her because of God,* he thought. He almost laughed at the irony, but it was too painful.

How could she do this? And on the Sunday before Christmas at that—the day he had planned to officially propose. Some celebration.

Thoughts of revenge entered his mind, something akin to refusing to do Jeffery's surgery unless she married him, but his pride wouldn't condone such an act. Besides, she might just agree that he shouldn't be involved with the surgery, and then where would he be? Lost and lonely like a character in a bad film. Dolefully, he stared at the Christmas decorations and shook his head. He hadn't felt so alone since the day Nicole had died on the train.

CHAPTER 16

When Bill arrived at the Plaza the next morning, he was greeted by Christmas music and bright decorations, and he had to stifle his urge to rip everything down. Barbara, one of the nurses on duty, took him aside. "Jeffery and his grandfather are here. They've been waiting a half hour already. They must really be anxious."

Bill glanced at his watch. No, he hadn't overslept. "Yeah, I guess. Have the people from *60 Minutes* showed up?"

"Not yet, but they called from a cell phone. They're on their way."

Then Bill asked the question to which he craved an answer, "Has Ms. Stuart called?"

"Not yet."

Feeling dejected, Bill went into his office and sat at the desk. He knew Kylee would be here shortly to support Jeffery, and they would have to face one another. But what was there left to say? She had made her choice. Would there be any way of convincing her to marry him? And if there was, what guarantee did he have that she would remain with him?

You know her better than that, a voice said in his head, but Bill wasn't sure. He didn't want comfort. He wanted to keep poking at his wounded heart until it was so numb that he couldn't feel any more pain.

Barbara appeared in the open doorway. "*60 Minutes* is here, and I've got Jeffery in the room. He wants to see you before he goes under."

Bill nodded and climbed to his feet. In the prep room, a camera man stood unobtrusively in the corner. "So are you ready?" he asked Jeffery.

The boy smiled faintly. "Yes. I think so."

"You're not nervous, are you?"

The smile grew larger. "I guess I am. Just a bit."

Mr. Rivers stood near his grandson, a comforting hand on his shoulder. "Don't you worry, Jeff. You're in good hands with Dr. Dubrey. Ms. Stuart says he's the best. He'll get you fixed up good."

"I'll do my best," Bill assured them. "And Dr. Bond, a burn specialist, will be here too. Now I'm going to wash up while they get you ready." He started to leave.

Jeffery's hand grabbed Bill's before he could walk away. "What if that ain't—isn't—good enough?" he asked. "Your best, I mean."

Bill turned back to the child, who stared at him with wide eyes. "It will be. Don't worry."

The boy glanced at his grandfather and then back at Bill, his ruined face innocent and helpless. "I know you're a good doctor and that you'll do good, but could you do one more thing for me?"

Bill stifled the irritation before it showed in his face. This experience was a new and scary thing for Jeffery, and he obviously needed any reassurance his doctor could give. "Sure, Jeff. May I call you Jeff?" The boy nodded solemnly. "I'll do it, if I can."

"Promise?"

Bill tried not to smile at his seriousness. "As long as it's not against the law and it's something I can do. Sure, I promise."

"Will you say a prayer before you start?" Jeffery asked, grabbing Bill's hand. "Gran'pa here says that the good Lord knows a lot of stuff that we don't, and so maybe He could help you."

"But I don't think—" Bill broke off. It wasn't up to him to tell Jeffery that *if* God existed, He was certainly too busy to care about such a small, insignificant thing as a burned child. So what could Bill say to Jeffery's request? What would he tell Jeffery if he were his son? What would Kylee tell him?

The thought made Bill's heart ache with uncertainty. Kylee believed that faith, especially the faith of a child, was a special thing. If it really was—and he trusted her judgment—could he destroy it? As a doctor, he knew that a patient's psychological outlook was directly connected to his well-being. But what if that child were well? Would the knowledge that God didn't care about anyone, much less a child, extinguish the light in a child's eye? Would the child ever be the same?

But the answers to these last questions wouldn't help him with Jeffery.

Mr. Rivers' eyebrows were drawn together tightly as though he wished he could make Jeffery take back the question. Not because he was embarrassed by it, but because he feared what Bill would say to his beloved grandson.

"Well, sure," Bill answered at last. "I'll say a prayer." He gently extracted the boy's hand from his own. "Now, you just relax and do what they tell you while I wash up. The next time you see me, the surgery will be over and you'll be well on your way to recovery. Don't worry, everything's going to be okay."

Bill left and after a short time Barbara followed, her face twisted in an amused smirk. "You pray? This I've got to see."

Bill snorted. "Yeah, right."

At that, her manner suddenly changed. She placed her hand firmly on her ample hips, and as she spoke her slight southern accent intensified. "Well, why not! You have to do it, you know. You promised, and in the two years I've worked here, I've never seen you break a promise. Will this be the first time? You'd think he asked you to jump off the Eiffel Tower. Goodness, Bill, it's just a prayer! Such a simple thing to give that poor child." She stalked off in disgust, leaving Bill in no doubt as to the strength of her feelings.

"What's gotten into her?" he muttered. He strode purposefully to the sink and scrubbed his hands vigorously, Barbara and Jeffery's words bouncing through his mind. He washed his hands three times before he finally made up his mind. "Well, I did promise Jeff, and it can't hurt."

Bill turned off the water and walked down the hall to his office. He shut the door. On second thought, he locked it. At first he was just going to mumble a few words to get it over with, but he had never been one for doing things partway. He had made a promise and he would keep it.

Feeling utterly stupid, he knelt by his chair. A fleeting memory of his mother came to mind, and how she had knelt with him by his bed each night when he was a child. "We kneel to show our submission," she had said in answer to his question. "So that He knows we respect His will, whatever that may be. And also so He knows we are thankful for everything He has given us."

"But if He's God, shouldn't He know already?" Bill had asked her.

"Yes, dear, but it helps us to tell Him, so we recognize how good He's been to us, and so that we will continue to choose good, which will make us happy. You see, everything God requires of us is for our benefit, not His. We are His children and He loves us."

Bill almost rolled his eyes at the memory. Instead, he closed them and began his prayer. "Jeff wants me to pray so I'm doing it. If someone hears this and even gives a—I mean if you care—you could help me help him during the surgery. He's a special kid and he's had a tough life, so he deserves it. That's it."

He knew it wasn't a good prayer, but it was his first prayer since Nicole had died. The intense warmth he had felt twice before entered his body, leaving him wondering. What was this feeling? He wished it would never stop.

There was a knock at the door and he lumbered awkwardly to his feet, expecting the feeling to leave, but it didn't.

"Ms. Stuart is here," Barbara said. "She's with Jeff. Dr. Bond is also here. Shall I tell them you're ready?"

"Yes, I just have to scrub again."

She gave him an odd look, but Bill only grinned at her silently until she vanished down the hall. He wasn't about to satisfy her curiosity. Somehow he felt that doing so would soil the new warmth in his soul. He didn't pretend to understand the odd feeling, but he wasn't prepared to let it go.

Bill saw Kylee only briefly before the surgery. She was leaning down, whispering something in Jeffery's good ear. The boy was nearly asleep, but his lips curled in a smile and then formed words Bill couldn't hear. For a moment Bill watched Kylee, her green eyes standing out against the short blonde hair. Her slightly upturned nose matched so well those adorable dimples on her cheeks—dimples that today were almost as nonexistent as her smile. Even so, she was full of life, youth, and exuberance, and he loved her.

She looked up and her gaze met his. Emotion flowed between them, silent, fierce, and all-consuming. Then Barbara appeared and ushered both Kylee and Mr. Rivers from the room.

* * * * *

Seeing Bill again made Kylee rehash the previous night's decision in her mind. She loved him and ached to be with him. She needed him. If only . . .

But no. She had prayed all night for a miracle, and was beginning to wonder if the Lord was fresh out. Kylee closed her eyes and repented for the thought. Many times she had cried to the Lord in the night after Emily had died, and questioning Him had never brought comfort. Only acceptance had eased her soul and given her the courage to continue a life that had appeared to have no meaning. Since then, she had found many things to live for.

As Kylee paced the halls waiting for the surgery to be over, Anna and Mrs. Johnson appeared for a follow-up interview by *60 Minutes*. The little girl's face was still swollen and red, but already looked much better than it had before the surgery twelve days earlier.

"Anna's a new girl," Mrs. Johnson said to Kylee. "Thank you for not giving up when those people . . ." She hugged Kylee. "You know."

"Yes, I do. And you're welcome." Kylee turned her attention to Anna.

"And now I'm waiting for Jeffery," Anna was saying to Deedra in front of the camera. The words were still somewhat distorted, but intelligible. "He's going to be my friend. I met him once before at the TV place."

"That'll be fun."

Anna nodded gravely. "And kids won't make fun of us." She briefly touched her upper lip.

Deedra finished her interview with Anna and came to stand by Kylee. "It's good to know you did the right thing by not giving up."

"It's not just me," Kylee said. "Look at all the support I'm getting from everyone." She told Deedra about the donations arriving in her P.O. box.

"That's great," Deedra said. "I'll make sure they mention it on the air. When people know others haven't given up on the sunken boat, they'll pitch in too. There's nothing like an underdog to spark community involvement. We'll have the Children's Hope yacht sailing in no time. You'll be able to help all the children you've ever wanted."

Kylee laughed, hoping Deedra was right. "Thank you so much."

"You're welcome." Deedra thumbed in the direction of the room where Bill was in surgery. "And that doctor's a good one. I hope you stick with him. Anyone can see he's crazy about you."

Kylee thought about what Deedra had said, and the chord it struck in her heart. But hadn't she given Bill ample opportunity to see things her way?

Her way.

Maybe she hadn't given Bill a real chance. Here she was, ready to bail out at the first sign of real trouble, to do anything to protect herself, hiding behind the excuse that it was God's will. But Bill was a good person, and he would find the truth eventually—she believed that with her whole heart. Maybe God's will, and also her good fortune, was to love Bill and help him find the truth, even if it took years. She didn't have to marry him, not right away, but she could ask him to simply search for the truth. If he would agree to that, the Lord would see to the rest. Regardless, she couldn't force him into believing. She could love and pray and hope, and most of all, be his friend. Then if they had to say goodbye in the end, she would know that she had given her best—her unconditional love.

Kylee blinked back the tears and silently thanked God for His inspiration, for she knew that this decision was much better than the one she had made in fear and anger. The road ahead might be long and hard, but she was accustomed to challenges, and Bill was worth a fight.

We were meant to meet. Kylee couldn't deny the thought. Bill had come around exactly when she needed him. Could she doubt that the Lord had sent him?

"Things have a way of working out." Suzy's words reverberated in Kylee's mind. *Yes. And I need to have faith that the Lord knows what He's doing.*

Kylee wished she could share her new insight with Bill, but knew that she wouldn't for many years to come—if ever. It would be enough to tell him she was willing to give their relationship time.

But would he search for the truth?

He loved her, yes, that she believed. But would he agree at least to learn about her faith? To understand it? To understand her? Maybe.

Kylee went to the waiting room to stay with Mr. Rivers. She found that Anna and Mrs. Johnson had disappeared with the *60 Minutes* crew and he was all alone. He smiled gratefully at her presence. Kylee returned the smile, but her thoughts stayed with Bill. She began to pray.

* * * * *

As Bill worked on Jeffery's skin grafts, assisted by the young burn specialist, Dr. Walter Bond, the warm feeling in his heart stayed with him. His fingers moved, fast and sure, as though they worked of their own accord. For the grafts, they used undamaged skin from Jeffery's own body, as well as donor skin. Bill marveled at the comparative ease of the procedure and the miracle of the human body.

Questions filtered into his mind. Was life only an accident? Did a creator exist—regardless of how indifferent or how loving? Bill was no longer sure. But the uncertainty didn't confuse him, nor did the way his hands moved so faultlessly to complete their work, almost as though he were being guided. Instead, it somehow comforted him. This feeling of being guided was not new, but it was the first time Bill acknowledged its existence and attributed it to a source other than himself. Could it be that a supreme being actually cared about this child and the other people Bill had helped with surgery? Was he an instrument in a grand design? This thought was new and almost frightening. How many times had Bill reveled in his own skill? How often had he felt pride at his ability to finish a surgery in the least amount of time with minimum complications and maximum results? How many times had he—as Kylee would say—trusted in the arm of flesh?

Had he been a tool all along? In the face of what was happening, Bill had to accept that the idea seemed logical. Actually, he had seen something similar happen at work. When he had too many patients to take care of, he used the Plaza staff to help out, requesting various tasks of them. In turn, he helped with their patients when needed. This not only accomplished the projects at hand, but also increased the skill of everyone involved. If a God existed, and if He really did care about His creations, would He not give them the ability and the desire to help each other? *I would do it that way,* Bill thought. Amazement and wonder flooded his heart, mind, and body. He had always thought that if he were to believe in a caring God the existence would have to be proven to him in a glaring, overt way—a miraculous cure for a patient with devastating complications, a vision of undeniable reality, a burned corpse returned to life. Never had he imagined this quiet realization that held so much power.

Bill knew then that he had lied when he told Kylee he had opened his heart. He hadn't, not to God anyway. Until now. Adrenaline coursed through Bill's veins. He felt like singing, dancing, and crying for joy. Was this incredible feeling why Kylee would risk their relationship? Oh, how much he had been missing!

The hours passed quickly and Bill's energy did not dim. When at last they were finished, Dr. Bond smiled at Bill. "You were amazing, Bill. I've never seen such great work. I learned a lot here today."

"You were pretty good yourself, Walter," Bill replied.

"I surprised myself." Dr. Bond glanced at Jeffery. "I think someone's looking out for that boy." His voice had become gruff and he turned away quickly, obviously embarrassed.

Bill put a hand on his shoulder. "Maybe you're right."

Barbara and the other nurse stared at him, but Bill ignored them and sauntered to the door. "You can take him to recovery. Let me know when he's awake."

Bill went to the waiting room to tell Mr. Rivers about the surgery. A nervous pit formed in his stomach as he saw Kylee sitting near the old man. He wanted to take her in his arms and confess that maybe he had been wrong, that he would do anything, believe anything, to have her in his life. But did Kylee love him for who he was, or was her love conditional upon his beliefs? He told himself it didn't matter, but he knew it did.

"Everything went smoothly," he told Mr. Rivers, who arose as he entered the waiting room. "Jeffery will be awake within a few hours or so and you can see him then."

"No complications?" Mr. Rivers asked quickly.

"None. It was a textbook surgery. He'll have the bandages for a while and we still have more work to do down the road, but providing the grafts take well, I think you and Jeff will be very pleased with the results."

"Thank you so much." Mr. Rivers took Bill's hand and pumped it up and down. "We can never repay you, but I know God will bless you."

Bill glanced at Kylee. "He might at that."

"Pardon me?" said Mr. Rivers. "I didn't hear you."

"Nothing. I'm just glad to have been able to help."

Bill was paged, and he reluctantly left Kylee and Mr. Rivers. There was so much he wanted to say to her, but he didn't know how to begin. Was what he had felt during the surgery real? He needed to find that out for himself. And most of all, he had to have Kylee in his life. He needed to know that she really loved him.

* * * * *

Minutes ticked slowly into hours. Bill didn't return and Kylee wondered what he was doing. Would he be back at all before she had to leave?

At last a nurse came into the waiting room. "Your grandson is awake," she said to Mr. Rivers. "Would you like to see him?"

"Yes, of course." The old man rose quickly to his feet.

"Can I come?" Kylee asked, hoping that, as at Anna's surgery, the family-only policy would be waived. Especially since Anna was anxious to see Jeffery and have her first real friend.

"Yes. I'm sure he'd like to see you too."

They were led into the recovery room. Bill wasn't present yet, though Kylee heard Barbara tell Mr. Rivers that he was on his way. Kylee and Mr. Rivers waited on each side of the bed as Jeffery's eyelids flickered. The left side of his face was completely covered with bandages, making him look small and helpless. Kylee leaned closer to him, taking his thin hand as Mr. Rivers had also done on the other side of the bed. The little boy opened his eyes sleepily, then blinked and focused on Kylee.

"Are you an angel?" he asked in a raspy voice, looking confused and more than a little alarmed.

"No, Jeffery. It's me, Kylee. How are you?"

"Oh, Kylee. I thought you were an angel. Like on TV."

"She is, Jeff."

Kylee turned at the voice and saw him in the doorway. "Bill."

He smiled at her with an expression she had never seen before, one she couldn't name. "I believe in angels now," he told her. "You're one. It's because of your persistence that we were able to do Jeff's surgery today." He looked at Jeffery. "I think that qualifies her to be an angel—at least to you."

"Her hair looks like a halo," Jeffery said, grinning weakly with the good half of his face.

"Yeah it does," Bill agreed.

Kylee laughed softly. "That's just the light reflecting off it." Whatever mood had struck Bill, Kylee was enjoying it. He was different somehow. Softer.

Jeffery's attention was diverted by the tears falling from his grandfather's eyes. "What's wrong, Gran'pa?"

"Nothing at all, boy. Nothing at all."

Kylee decided to leave them alone together and excused herself. Her heart thumped erratically when Bill followed close behind.

"Bill—" she began at the same time he said, "Kylee." He nodded for her to go first.

"We need to talk."

"I agree. But my next patient's waiting and has been for the last half-hour. Could we get together later tonight?"

Kylee was relieved that the hurt and anger she had seen in him the night before was no longer apparent. "I'd like that."

"Your place or mine?"

"I have some work to do out your way for Children's Hope, so I could stop by your condo. Just tell me a time."

"Six?" He led her to his office and pulled a set of keys out of the drawer. "Better take these, though, in case I'm late. Sometimes my appointments run over."

"I'll make us dinner."

"You don't have to."

She touched his arm. "I know."

With no warning, his arms went around her and pulled her tight. "I love you, Kylee Stuart." He kissed her hard on the mouth before drawing away. "See you tonight."

Kylee watched him leave, her senses reeling at his kiss, at the strength of their mutual attraction. So much for just being friends until she could help him find his faith. And what would she do if that never happened? She couldn't imagine living without him, or living without sharing a belief in God. Yet she sensed a difference in him; maybe he had already begun soul searching. Maybe she simply had to exercise her faith as she had at Emily's death. Back then, her terrible loss and pain had been transformed into hope and joy; it could be so again.

But why this sense of unease? Why this dread? She had not felt such a tangible fear since Raymond packed his bags and left.

CHAPTER 17

Kylee let herself into Bill's condo at five and began dinner preparations, glad that Bill had taught her how to program the oven. As the roast was cooking, she wandered around, looking for signs of Bill's real self, something that would tell her what was in his heart. But everything she saw could belong to anyone, except for the Christmas decorations she had put up and the crude drawing of his parents on the wall in the sitting room.

The drawing reminded Kylee of the others Bill had shown her before. She went upstairs and into the exercise room where the drawings were still spread out on the floor. But there were more this time, new ones she had never seen. In two, Bill had drawn Anna and Jeffery as they had looked at the TV station. Anna was clinging to a hand, presumably her mother's, and Jeffery stared at his lap, his face slightly turned as though to hide his burns. From each stroke she could see into Bill's heart, and she knew why he had agreed to help the children. Somehow it meant a reemerging of the old Bill, the Guillaume Debré who had fled France with such vengeance. The children had given him a way to heal the past.

Most of the additional drawings were of Kylee, and again the lines told of his deep sorrow for hurting her, and of his profound love. There was something eternal in the drawings, something almost celestial. A reason to live, a reason to believe. *If I had seen these, I would never have doubted him,* she thought. The road before her might not be easy, but he was worth it.

She gathered the drawings, old and new, and carefully arranged them in the box. Though cumbersome, the box wasn't too heavy for

Kylee to carry downstairs. She placed them on the coffee table in the sitting room and began to thumb through them again, feeling close to Bill and more in love with him every moment.

A timer went off and she wandered into the kitchen to check on dinner. It was nearing six, but Bill still hadn't arrived. *Maybe I'll watch a little TV.* Returning to the sitting room, Kylee settled on the couch and flipped the TV on with the remote. There was a blanket folded neatly on the couch, and she spread it over her. Before long, her eyes grew heavy.

The phone rang, jerking her out of sleep. "Hello?" she asked breathlessly when she had finally found the source of the noise.

"Kylee, it's me."

"Hi, Bill."

"You sound odd. Have you been sleeping?"

Kylee yawned. "Yes, actually. I guess I didn't realize how tired I am. It's been a long month, you know. So when are you coming?"

"Well, I've been delayed by an emergency. Nothing too serious, but I have to stay and take care of it. I've got at least another hour here, plus the twenty minute drive. I should be there by at least seven-thirty, eight at the latest. Will you wait for me? I wouldn't ask, but I really need to see you."

"Don't worry, I'll wait. I've already been to see Chantel's parents—you know, the baby with Apert syndrome—to talk with them about scheduling a surgery, and beyond that I had nothing else to do. Dinner will be cold, but I'll reheat it. Until you get here I'll just doze on your couch."

"Are you sure you don't mind?"

"No." She paused and swallowed hard before adding, "And, Bill, I love you, too."

"You don't know what that means to me to hear you say that."

She picked up one of the drawings he had made of her dressed in her bronze and gold evening dress. *I think maybe I do.*

They said good-bye, and after turning off the oven, Kylee curled back up on the couch and was soon asleep.

Only a short time later, she heard the shrill cry of the fire alarm. Groggily she climbed to her feet. She could smell the smoke as it began to fill the room, black and billowing, blotting out the overhead light. How long had the smoke alarm been sounding? And where was the fire? She looked around but the smoke made it difficult to see; and the darkness increased with every moment.

All her sleepiness vanished. *I have to get out of here!* She was nearly to the sitting room doorway when she remembered Bill's drawings. *I can't leave them! They're all he has of Nicole.* Taking a few steps back, she grabbed the box and rushed into the entryway. There were no flames that she could see, but the area was also filled with black smoke that stung her eyes and throat. Blinking to ease the stinging, she held her breath as she ran to the front door.

There was no one outside, but she could hear screams coming from a neighboring apartment. She watched, stunned, as people began stumbling from the surrounding condos in a seemingly endless chaotic stream. Flames flickered in windows of the two condos directly to the right of Bill's, and smoke surged from five or six others.

Kylee placed Bill's box of drawings on top of her car, and leaned against it to collect her scattered wits. Then she remembered the drawing Bill had made of his parents, and his poignant expression when he told her it was the only picture he had of them.

Without thinking twice, Kylee ran back into the condo. The entryway and sitting room were still dense with smoke, but this time she noticed flames dancing on Bill's entertainment center and the surrounding wall, crackling as they eagerly devoured everything they touched. *Must have spread from the neighbor's,* she thought. Even as she watched, sparks jumped to the couch where she had been lying only minutes earlier.

Hastily, she grabbed the drawing on the wall and made for the door. The thick smoke entered her lungs and she coughed and tripped over the blanket she had left on the floor. A sharp pain filled her head as she fought to remain conscious.

* * * * *

The clock in his BMW told Bill it was after eight. He drove rapidly through the dark streets as he headed for home and Kylee. Kylee! She would be waiting for him. She might be asleep, but she would be waiting.

With a smile he recalled the last time he had seen her sleeping on a couch. He had loved Nicole at the time, as he would always love her, but something about Kylee had touched him even then. In the almost two months since she had come back into his life she had changed him, had given him a reason for living. She had evoked in him an incredible happiness when he had thought those emotions gone forever. He had been wrong about a lot of things.

As he approached the block of his gated community, he saw a dark cloud rising in the air, lit by a strange light that didn't come from the street lamps. A chilling dread fell upon his shoulders, reaching out a claw-like hand for his heart, and for an instant, he saw Nicole again, black in his arms.

Shoving the agonizing vision aside, he drove like a man possessed through the gate and over to his street. Horror flooded his senses as he saw the whole row of condominiums where he lived awash in flames.

Kylee!

The scream ripped silently through his head and heart and soul. When he had last talked to her she had been nearly asleep on the couch. Was she still there? Had her dinner caught fire while she slept?

He remembered the dream of holding a burned Nicole in his arms, only to look down on her face and find that it was Kylee. In that same dream he had dropped her and run away.

She has to be okay!

He left his car down the street, and ran to the crowd gathered by the growing blaze that lit the evening sky. Sirens wailed in the background. By the light of the fire he urgently searched for Kylee's pixie face, her golden halo of hair.

Nothing.

He grabbed people from behind, turning them to face him, but none were Kylee.

Oh dear God!

He prayed as he had never prayed before. That morning during Jeffery's surgery, he had understood that God did exist. If God had cared about Jeffery's surgery enough to help Bill with the surgery, He could also save Kylee.

But Kylee wasn't in the crowd, nor did she emerge from the raging inferno that was now his home. The front door gaped open as if mocking Bill's despair.

It's all my fault!

He wanted to cry and scream out the unfairness of it all. This was too much! He had already lost the first woman he loved to flames—to bear another such burden was beyond his ability. The sirens were louder now, as they had been on that day in France, but Bill knew they would come too late for Kylee.

I couldn't save Nicole, he thought. *There was nothing I could do. But I can save Kylee—or die trying.* Death seemed nothing when compared to losing her.

A thought came, unbidden, but not unwelcome. Was this how Jesus had felt when He had atoned for the sins of the world? Did He love so much that His own welfare was of no concern?

Bill ran toward his condo, but two men held him back. "Are you crazy?" someone asked.

"She's in there. I have to get her out!"

The men wouldn't release him. "No one's in there," one said.

"Or if they are it's too late," added the other.

"Let the fire department handle it," an old lady in the crowd told him. "Look at those flames. You might not get back out."

Bill knew that, but he also knew that Kylee was inside. He felt her presence there as certainly as if he could see through the wall. "Let me go!" He flung off their arms with a strength he had never felt before, and darted to his open door. "Kylee!" he shouted. "Kylee!"

No answer.

Red and orange flames licked the sides of the entryway and roared in the hall that had once led to the sitting room. The Christmas decorations on the stair railing were a smoldering mess, and at the sight fear stabbed through him. He recalled vividly the day he had been burned on the train: the putrid smell of cooking flesh, the biting, pervasive smoke that filled his lungs and nostrils, the choking and the helplessness. How badly it had hurt! What agony he had endured! And that was even before he had learned Nicole was dead.

Bill was aware that his hands shook, that his flesh cringed at the thought of the fire eating its way through his body. But visions of saving Kylee were stronger. He had run away once before when Elaina and Troy had taken off with the charity money, and once again in his dream, but there was no way he would leave her now. Let the fire destroy him as it had destroyed his life once before. So long as Kylee was saved, nothing else mattered.

Bill tore off his jacket and threw it over his head. Taking a deep breath, he plunged into the roaring wall of flame. The jump lasted only a second, but to his fear-filled mind it was an eternity. On the other side of the flames, he sank weakly to his knees, unable to see through the thick smoke that stung his eyes and nose. His shirt and pants felt hot against his skin.

Fighting panic, he staggered blindly toward the couch. *Please, dear God in Heaven,* he begged.

Halfway to the couch his foot hit something soft. Bending swiftly, he crouched and reached out with his hands. It was Kylee—or at least he assumed it was her. He gathered the limp body into his arms, unsure if she was breathing. His hand touched a blanket and he wrapped her into it. Coughing dryly and fighting dizziness, he struggled to the door, the body in his arms growing heavier. Again he leapt through the angry wall of flames.

He stumbled and went down on one knee, but he forced himself to his feet again. His stinging eyes teared so much that he couldn't see the door to the outside, but he knew where it was. Blindly, he reached the doorway and staggered out into the night.

The sudden rush of December air was cool and welcome against his seared flesh and sore throat. He gulped the fresh air and tried to take another step forward, but an excruciating pain ate at his back and his legs refused to work. As he sank to the ground, he was aware of someone taking the lifeless body from his arms, but the realization came from far away, as though in a distorted dream. He tried to hold onto Kylee, but someone knocked him to the ground. Then he was being rolled across the grass, pain filling his senses.

"Please, is she all right?" he begged.

No one answered.

"Tell me!" he screamed.

Agony ate at his consciousness, and abruptly everything went dark.

* * * * *

The first thing Bill became aware of was the terrible pain in his back. It was all-encompassing, filling every thought and particle of his being. It was a barrier beyond which he could see and feel nothing.

Gradually, other things penetrated the barrier. He found he was lying on his side in a bed. He could hear someone talking quietly. A woman's voice.

Remembrance came back to him. "Kylee," he moaned. "Kylee!"

Was she dead?

Not knowing was a worse pain than what he felt from his back, yet at the same time the uncertainty at least allowed a slim hope. A terrible, desperate, longing kind of hope that made Bill weep.

A soft hand wiped a tear on his cheek. "Bill, I'm here."

His eyes blinked open abruptly. "Kylee?"

"Yes, it's me."

With difficulty, his eyes focused through the pain. She sat in a wheelchair near his bed, her hair hanging limply around her pale, haggard face. "Am I in heaven?" he asked. "I have never seen you so beautiful." He reached for her hand, and renewed pain shot through his body. He groaned, "Oh, it can't be heaven. It hurts too much."

Kylee chuckled softly. "You're in the hospital. We both are, only I'm being released today. You, however, will be staying a few more weeks."

From the pain he felt, Bill believed her. "What day is it?" he asked.

"Christmas Eve."

"I've been asleep that long?"

Kylee's smile faded and an abject expression took possession of her face. "They tell me you've been in and out, but not really aware. It was touch and go for a while."

Bill let that information digest before asking, "What happened? It was my stove, wasn't it? I should have known better than to buy one like that."

"Your stove?" Her brows furrowed in puzzlement.

"That started the fire. It short-circuited or something."

"Oh, no. Actually, the fire started at that older couple's house next door to you. Mrs. Simpton was making some Christmas candy for the neighbors and she went to deliver a batch she had made earlier and forgot about it. The candy burned and the curtains caught fire. By the time she returned it was too late. Her whole place was ablaze."

"Was anyone hurt?"

Kylee shook her head. "Her husband was at their church building, doing some cleaning, and the neighbors got out in time."

"Except for you."

She grimaced. "I know it was stupid, but I went back for something. I didn't think the fire would take over so rapidly. But I guess it got a good head start on me, coming like it did from the Simptons."

"Who would imagine such devastation from a batch of Christmas candy?" Bill was relieved that his stove was not the cause, but even more relieved that no one else had been hurt. "So what did you go back for?"

The way her mouth pursed, Bill knew she didn't want to tell him.

"Well?" he insisted.

"The drawing you made of your parents."

He frowned. "You shouldn't have done that. It wasn't important enough to risk your life for. *Nothing* in the condo was worth that."

"I know," she gave a deep sigh and tears invaded her former calm. "It burned anyway. I almost killed us both for nothing. I'm sorry."

"That sketch means nothing compared to your life. I can draw another one."

She leaned her face close to his, gripping his hand tightly. "Oh, Bill, I'd thought I'd lost you! I've never prayed so hard in my entire life."

"Me too." Bill spoke the words simply, but they were not wasted on Kylee.

"I knew you'd understand one day," she said. "And I was ready to wait for that for however long it took."

Her lips trembled and Bill had never wanted to kiss her more than he did at that moment. He turned his head and kissed her fiercely, ignoring the additional pain that rippled through his body. "I love you, Kylee. I love you so much. When I thought you were dead, I went crazy. And then the sight of the fire inside the house almost paralyzed me. I thought I couldn't make it through to you. I—I was terrified . . ."

Her cheek rested against his. "It's over now. The doctor said that in another minute it might have been too late for me. You saved my life."

Bill felt tears on his face but was unsure if they were his own. "You *are* my life." He kissed her again and she responded fervently. Against her soft lips, he murmured, "So does this mean you'll marry me?"

She gave a soft laugh. "If you insist. But first you'll have to get out of here." Her eyes briefly wandered the room and lingered on the Christmas wreath tacked to the door. "I guess this isn't really where we had imagined spending our first Christmas together."

"Are you kidding? I don't mind." Bill paused, searching for the words to describe to her the feeling of gratitude and love in his heart. "This is the best Christmas ever, Kylee. One I will never forget. It's the first time I understood why anyone would be willing to give his life for another—especially on a cross. It's the first time I understand why God cares about His creations, His children."

Tears trickled down her cheeks and her voice trembled. "Because of love."

"Yes, because of love."

There was more, but Bill could not voice it. Perhaps one day he would be able to capture the feeling in his art—to draw how understanding the reasoning behind the Savior's crucifixion had helped him set aside the burden of his own self-inflicted cross, the one he had carried since Nicole's death. For some incomprehensible reason, his life had been saved on that fiery train, and he was finally headed toward fulfilling that purpose. Now he could quit living in the past . . . and hiding from the future.

He could forgive himself.

He met Kylee's eyes again, her face full of a love that his fingers itched to replicate. Someday soon he would draw her looking at him this way. He would burn this very moment into his memory and onto the paper, and it would become the beginning. The future was theirs.

Rachel Ann Nunes (pronounced *noon-esh)* knew she was going to be a writer when she was thirteen years old. She now writes five days a week in a home office with constant interruptions from her five young children. One of her favorite things to do is to take a break from the computer and build a block tower with her two youngest. Several of her children have begun their own novels, and they have fun writing and plotting together.

Rachel enjoys traveling, camping, spending time with her family, and reading. She served an LDS mission to Portugal. She and her husband, TJ, and their children live in Utah Valley, where she is a popular speaker for religious and writing groups. *This Very Moment* is her twelfth novel to be published by Covenant. Her *Ariana* series is a best-seller in the LDS market.

Rachel enjoys hearing from her readers. You can write to her at P.O. Box 353, American Fork, UT 84003-0353, send e-mail to rachel@rachelannnunes.com, or visit her website at http://www.rachelannnunes.com.

AN EXCERPT FROM MICHELE ASHMAN BELL'S

Written in the Stars

Taking a sheet from the laundry basket, Michaela Reynolds folded it in half as she glanced at the television before her. Although she'd turned it on mostly for company while she folded clothes that evening, she'd become interested in the romantic comedy.

She stopped for a moment to watch as the couple on the screen sailed off into the sunset, their sailboat cutting gracefully through gentle waves, the colors on the horizon blazing red, orange and purple as the sun sank lazily into an azure blue ocean. Romantic music played as the boat grew smaller and smaller.

She hugged the sheet to her chest, and her thoughts drifted away. To feel the fresh ocean breeze . . . the gentle motion of the waves . . . to sail away to an exotic island . . . away from all the cares in the world . . . to be so deeply in love . . .

It seemed so long ago that she and her husband, Ben, had ever been that in love. She wondered what had happened. How had everything changed right under her nose?

"Mom!" The voice of her six-year-old daughter, Jordan, broke into her trance. "Zach has a stinky diaper."

It took a moment for reality to return. Michaela wanted to stay in her daydream, inside the boat, feeling the warmth of the sun on her face. And more than anything, she wanted for Ben and her to be like they used to be—putting each other first, doing little thoughtful acts of love for each other, facing life's challenges together, side by side.

"Oh, yuck. It's everywhere!" Jordan yelled again.

This was eighteen-month-old Zachary's fifth day with diarrhea, and it still wasn't getting better. He'd gotten it from his twin brother,

Gabriel, who'd had it last week. Michaela wondered if she should take him to the doctor again.

Hurrying into the playroom, she was greeted with the overwhelming stench of a messy diaper and a smiling Zachary, who was standing in a puddle on the carpet that had just been steam cleaned.

"Poo-poo," he said with pride. He lifted one leg and smiled at his mother. Gabriel was playing with a little plastic fire truck and happily running its wheels through the puddle.

Fighting the urge to flee to her bedroom and hide, wishing her husband could be home early just once during the week, Michaela scooped up Zachary, threw a towel over the soiled spot and ran to the bathtub, with Gabriel following close at her heels. She deposited Zach in the tub, where he immediately set to playing with his Sesame Street tub toy, giggling as his mother attempted to remove his soiled clothes and diaper. Gabe whined because he wanted to get in the tub with his brother, but Michaela wouldn't let him.

Jordan, who'd discovered the mess in the first place, poked her head in to see what was going on. "Oooh, stinky. Can I have a fruit snack, Mommy?"

"Sure," Michaela answered. "Hand me that washcloth, sweetie. And get a fruit snack for Gabe, please."

Jordan gave her the washcloth and skipped off to get the snacks. Michaela was grateful that Jordan was such a mellow child because the twins were a handful. Actually, they were two handfuls and completely out of control. One or the other of them was usually into something—either pulling all the books off the bookshelves, dumping boxes of cereal onto the kitchen floor, unloading the cupboards in the bathroom, or drawing on the walls with pens and markers that could always be found, no matter how well Michaela kept them hidden and out of their reach.

She scrubbed Zach with soap and rinsed him off, then pulled him out of the tub. Wrapping him in a towel, she whisked him off to his room to get him diapered and ready for bed. She lived for bedtime. It was the only time she had to herself—when the kids were asleep.

"Mom!" another voice wailed. "You shrunk my jeans!"

Michaela closed her eyes and prayed for strength. Her twelve-year-old daughter, Lauryn, was probably her biggest challenge.

Lauryn knew exactly which buttons to push, and she pushed them often. Michaela would rather change five of Zach's dirty diapers than deal with one of Lauryn's emotional outbursts.

Lauryn had reached the age when the acceptance of her peers was more important than anything. She had to have the right clothes, the right hairstyle, the right makeup. Everything had to be perfect or her life was miserable. And when Lauryn's life was miserable, so was everyone else's.

Michaela worried about her twelve-year-old, who already had the body of a fourteen- or fifteen-year-old. Remembering back upon her own youth, Michaela hadn't really grown and matured until the summer after her eighth-grade year. Lauryn's body had matured early, but her emotions and coping skills were still those of a twelve-year-old. Lauryn took after Ben's side of the family with her honey-colored hair, hazel green eyes, and smooth, creamy skin. She was also built like Ben's side of the family, long-legged and tall. All the boys at school seemed to have suddenly taken notice of her, which wasn't helping.

"Honey, I didn't even dry them," Michaela hollered back. "Zach, hold still!" Zach loved to run around without any clothes on, as did his twin brother. The other kids got a kick out of watching them streak naked through the house.

But Michaela was in no mood tonight to chase naked babies around the house or deal with a pair of shrunken jeans. In fact, if these kids didn't get to bed soon, she wouldn't be able to guarantee their safety. She'd had it with all of them!

"Mom!" Lauryn whined. "I wanted to wear those jeans to school tomorrow."

"Go throw them in the washer again, and I'll try to stretch them out for you," Michaela yelled, trying to keep the irritation from creeping into her voice.

"Mom," another voice yelled, this one from her son, Isaac. "I'm running over to Brandon's house to do my math."

She glanced at her watch. It was almost nine. "Don't be late."

"I won't," he replied, clearly annoyed. The door slammed and Zach started to cry. He lived to go outside, especially when his big brother was out there.

"Come on, let's get you a bottle," Michaela told Zach, who stopped wailing at the offer and sniffled.

While Lauryn stomped down the hallway to her bedroom and slammed the door shut, Michaela quickly filled two bottles with milk. She really needed to wean the twins, but she was as attached to their bottles as they were. It was the only way she could get the beds made in the morning or dinner made in the evening. At least they'd sit and drink their bottles and watch Barney for half an hour. She laid Zach in his bed with his stuffed dog, Woofy, and grabbed Gabe, who was in the bathroom dipping fruit snacks in the toilet before eating them.

"Gabe, honey," she scolded. "No, no."

"No, no!" he yelled back and ran for the door.

Michaela caught him and carried him kicking and screaming to his room. She laid him in bed with his bottle, and he immediately curled up with his Pooh Bear. Michaela released a weary sigh. Who needed aerobics when she had active twin sons?

From the instant she had brought the twins home, everyone's lives had been drastically altered by their presence in the home. At first, Michaela had hoped to continue teaching piano lessons, but with twins in the house, reality struck her with the force of a Mac truck, and she'd had to tell her twelve students to find another teacher. Not that the twins weren't worth it, but she had loved teaching piano, using her background in music to help young children develop a love for music. At times she missed the fulfillment teaching had provided her. She hoped that someday she would be able to resume teaching, but that day seemed so far away.

"Mommy," Jordan called from the family room. "The carpet's all squooshy and wet."

"What?" Michaela shut the door to the twins' room and went to see what Jordan was talking about.

"The carpet's—"

Walking into the family room, Michaela screamed, scaring Jordan to tears. Sure enough, the carpet was soaked. The water appeared to be coming from the laundry room.

"Lauryn!" Michaela yelled at the top of her lungs, running for the washer. "Jordan, please stop crying." As she opened the lid to the washer, she heard footsteps pounding down the hallway.

"What!" her daughter said with a huff of annoyance.

"Look what you've done!" Michaela demanded, angry tears blurring her vision. The washer was so packed with jeans, towels, and bedding that the agitator couldn't move. Lauryn would have had to jump on the load to pack it in so tightly. Water was spilling out over the top where the washer was trying to fill the tub but couldn't saturate the contents.

Michaela quickly shut off the washer. "Put Jordan to bed," she commanded.

Lauryn opened her mouth to respond but clamped it shut again. Taking one look at her mother's face, she quickly obeyed.

Grabbing dry towels out of the nearest bathroom, Michaela packed the threshold going out of the laundry room to prevent more water from seeping onto the carpet. Inside the laundry room, water slowly emptied through the drain on the floor. She removed some of the items from the washer and then started the cycle over, knowing she would have dozens of towels to wash after she soaked up the water in the family room.

Irritated with herself for not buying the wet/dry vacuum at Costco that she'd wanted, Michaela moved the couch and rocker out of the way and laid towels all along the baseboards. Her husband, Ben, hadn't felt they could afford the vacuum, not with their oldest son, Jared, on a mission in Argentina.

Michaela began stepping on the towels to soak up the water. As soon as one towel was completely wet, she replaced it with another dry towel and continued the process. Sweat formed on her brow as she worked to get the water up as quickly as possible. Right in the middle of the disaster cleanup, the phone rang. She let it ring three times, thinking Lauryn would answer it, but finally on the fourth ring she reached for the phone herself.

"This is Neva Patterson. Is the bishop home?" an elderly voice asked.

"No," Michaela answered breathlessly. "He's at the church."

"Oh, dear," Sister Patterson said. "I need to talk to him right away."

"Why don't you try calling over at the church?" she suggested, with as much patience as she could muster. As often as Sister Patterson called, Michaela thought the woman would know her husband's schedule by now.

"Do you happen to have that number?" the woman asked.

Michaela was up to her eyeballs in soggy towels, and the last thing she felt like doing was playing "information" for ward members. "Just a minute," she said, finding the ward list and giving Sister Patterson the number for their church building.

Somewhat pacified, the older woman hung up and Michaela went back to work.

It wasn't enough that her husband, Ben, worked long hours as a broker training specialist for Hampton & Gibb, which took him out of town three or four times a month. For the last two years he had also been bishop of their ward. Both jobs were so demanding that he was rarely home, and his absence was felt in every aspect of his family's lives. With all the challenges at work and the constant demands from their ward, Michaela and the kids had gradually become used to being shoved onto the back burner. In fact, they'd been placed there so many times, they hardly bothered to include him in their activities anymore; it saved the energy of being disappointed or waiting anxiously for him to show up. They didn't like having him gone, but they'd been forced to adjust.

"What's going on?" It was Isaac, just getting back from his friend's house. He stood at the doorway as Michaela gathered up the last batch of wet towels off the carpet. It wasn't dry by any means, but it was as good as she could get it.

"The washer overflowed," she told him wearily, spraying carpet cleaner on the carpet where Zach had had his accident.

He pulled a face. "Do you need some help?"

She appreciated the offer; Isaac was a pretty thoughtful kid, when he wasn't wrapped up in himself. "I just need to get the fan from the basement and turn it on to help the carpet dry," she said, scrubbing the spot on the carpet until the stain was gone.

"I'll go get it," he offered.

"Thanks," she replied, with an appreciative smile.

She loaded another batch of towels into the washer and folded the batch that came out of the dryer, making sure to pull Lauryn's jeans out and stretch them while they were wet. She didn't want to wake up to another crisis, especially after tonight.

Isaac came upstairs with the fan and plugged it in, angling it toward the wet carpet. Just then the phone rang.

"Can you get it?" Michaela requested. "If it's Sister Patterson, tell her your dad still isn't home." She glanced at her watch and noticed it was almost eleven. Her husband usually got home around ten-thirty or so, but something must have held him up at the church. As usual.

"Mom," Isaac said. "It's for you."

She stuck her head out of the laundry room and mouthed, "Who is it?" to him.

He shrugged and set the phone on the counter. "I'm going to bed," he said.

Michaela pushed the straggly wisps of hair off her face as she walked to the phone. All she wanted to do was go to bed and escape.

"Hello?" she asked, wondering which member of the ward was in urgent need of her husband now.

"Mikki?" a woman's voice said. The voice sounded vaguely familiar.

"Yes?" Michaela answered, searching her memory for a name to fit the voice.

"Mikki, this is Chelsie. Chelsie Powell."

"Chelsie! Omigosh, how are you?" Michaela exclaimed, collapsing onto a bar stool. She hadn't talked to Chelsie for months, and had forgotten that she and her husband, Nathaniel, were moving back to town after living in Switzerland. "Where are you?"

"We're finally back, Mikki. I couldn't wait to call so I took a chance you were still up." Chelsie's voice held a mixture of fatigue and excitement. She and her husband had originally planned to stay in Switzerland for two years, but then Nathaniel had a chance to transfer back to the states. Chelsie, homesick for family and friends, had begged him to take it. When Chelsie and Nathaniel had first moved to Switzerland, Michaela remembered thinking how fun and adventurous it sounded to live in a foreign country like that. Chelsie and her husband didn't have children yet, so it was easier for them to move overseas.

"I'm glad you're back," Michaela told her. "I've missed you."

"I've missed you, too," her friend replied. "Have you talked to Jocelyn lately?"

"Not since Christmas. She's so busy with her travel business I hardly see her anymore."

"I can imagine. I tried to call her, too, but she's in San Francisco right now. She'll be home this weekend, and that's partly why I called. We need to get together and go out to dinner so we can catch up on what everyone's been doing."

Michaela didn't tell her friend that her life wasn't worth catching up on, but she was all for having an evening away from home with her friends. "Whatever is good for you and Jocelyn, just let me know," she said, trying to cover a yawn that sneaked up on her. It had been a long day and she was tired, too tired, in fact to shower before going to bed, even though her shirt was uncomfortably damp from her earlier exertions.

"I'll call you back after I talk to her. Hey, are you okay?" Chelsie's voice softened. "You don't sound good."

It was just like Chelsie to pick up on it, Michaela thought. The two women had been friends since grade school, and even with the passage of time and Chelsie's travels with her husband, they were still as close now as they had been growing up. Jocelyn remained a good friend as well, although her work schedule kept her busy. Chelsie, Michaela, and Jocelyn had been inseparable through high school and had even roomed together their first year of college. Then Jocelyn met Sean and the two had married. Chelsie and Michaela had remained roommates and finished another year of college, then Chelsie had gone on a mission.

Michaela had also considered going on a mission, and if it hadn't been for Ben, she would have. The two of them had dated in high school, and then continued to date after Ben had served his mission in England. The bishop of Michaela's student ward had counseled her to not put a mission before marriage, so she hadn't, although sometimes she wondered how much different her life would be if she had gone.

"I'm just tired," Michaela said. "It's been a busy day."

"Then I'll let you go. But we'll talk again soon, okay?"

Michaela hung up the phone, glad that Chelsie was back. She and Jocelyn were like the sisters she never had. Her two older brothers were great, but it wasn't like having a sister. She couldn't call her brothers and tell them how hard some days were—how difficult it was to take care of the children by herself, how often her prayers were pleas for forgiveness for her resentment toward Ben's clients and the ward members who saw her husband more than her family did. Worst of all was the guilt she felt on those days she wondered if it was all worth it, especially when her husband no longer seemed to have the time or patience to listen to her needs and feelings. He was too burned out from hearing everyone else's problems.

Michaela and Ben had always had a happy, loving relationship. From those first weeks after they'd met, she'd considered him her best friend. He was friendly and outgoing, and people were naturally drawn to him, which was why he was such a success with his job, training other brokers in offices around the country, and also why he was so good in his ward calling, especially with the youth.

But as good as he was doing with everyone else, Michaela had been thinking that she and Ben weren't doing so well. They seemed to drift further and further apart as daily life intruded upon them. They had six children with busy lives, and Michaela had her hands full keeping the home functioning smoothly; Ben had a demanding career, and his church calling took nearly every spare minute that he wasn't traveling.

Michaela knew that divorce wasn't the answer. She and Ben had decided when they'd married that divorce wasn't an option. They were committed to each other, they had made temple covenants and promises to each other, and they would work through their problems together.

Still, she kept picturing how it would be when the children grew up and moved away. She could see Ben and herself as complete strangers. Two people with nothing in common, nothing to say to each other. Two people who didn't even know each other anymore.

And the thought troubled her.